SACRAMENTO PUBLIC LIBRARY
828 "I" STREET
SACRAMENTO, CA 95814

8/2018

D0468872

The Golden Virgin

Zenigata Heiji Mystery Stories

KODO NOMURA

SHELLEY MARSHALL (TRANSLATOR)

Zenigata Heiji Mystery Stories

The Golden Virgin

www.jpopbooks.com

Copyright © 2018 Shelley Marshall

All rights reserved.

ISBN: 978-1718803152
ISBN-10: 171880315X

CONTENTS

CHAPTER ONE

THE GOLDEN VIRGIN

1

"HEIJI, I HAVE A SPECIAL FAVOR to ask of you. Will you accept?"

"Yes."

Zenigata Heiji had difficulty deciphering his true motives and furtively glanced up at the stern but handsome man of twenty-four or -five years old, who was sitting with his knees covered by a lined kimono specked with small indigo dots. The man gently placed a hand, accustomed to playing with a *yazo* balancing toy, on the floor in front of him.

"In the worst case, Magistrate Asakura Iwami-no-kami-sama will be the instrument for harakiri on behalf of the shogun's Council of Elders. I can't force you, Heiji, but will you risk your life to do this for me?" asked Sasano Shinsaburo, the police sergeant of the Minami-cho magistrate. He was a man said to be the personal adviser to Magistrate Asakura Iwami-no-kami and possessed a mysterious noble appearance and physique.

"Whatever you wish. Sir, if this matter is important to the man who performed many favors for my father, I don't have enough lives to give. Please, tell me everything," said Heiji.

As Heiji stepped up to the parlor, Shinsaburo slid off the floor cushion as a signal to invite him inside and said, "The shogun has announced another falconry hunt in Zoshigaya."

"What?"

"You probably heard about the disturbance during the last hunt there."

"I know a little about it."

Heiji had heard about the incident. When Iemitsu, the third Tokugawa shogun, released a falcon near Kishimojin in Zoshigaya, an arrow came out of nowhere and flew dangerously close to the top of his shoulder. It glided into the metal backing of his *jingasa* camp helmet bearing the hollyhock family crest of the Tokugawa, and dropped to the ground three paces before his eyes.

The search for the scoundrel began at once, but he got away.

Later investigations revealed the deep penetration into the falcon's wing of the arrow up to its shaft and a variety of wolfsbane poison known as *torikabuto*, used by the Ainu people of Matsumae, smeared on the polished white, two-inch arrowhead.

Shinsaburo said, "Although the villain is still on the loose, the shogun announced he would go out on another falconry hunt in Zoshigaya. Of course, the Council of Elders, as well as his advisers, offered various objections. But in line with his normal disposition, once the shogun made his announcement, he would never alter his plans. As a result, the Council of Elders made a direct request to Asakura Iwami-no-kami-sama to hunt down this villain who dared to shoot a long-distance arrow at the shogun by the day of the falconry hunt. What do you think would be a good strategy?"

This generation's man of ability, Sasano Shinsaburo, relied on Heiji with his bearing of a police detective as well as his mind.

Shinsaburo said, "You've told me quite a lot. Officer Miyori, Heiji will be in charge, so please hide nothing and tell him everything you think I would want to know."

"Of course, please feel free to ask questions about anything you don't understand," said the officer.

Heiji said, "All right, I have a question. Could you tell me exactly why the shogun is drawn to Zoshigaya for falconry? I'm asking because few small birds live there. This fall, the opinion is game animals are in abundance in Meguro and Kirigaya."

"Now, there's no need to raise your voice."

"Yes, well, I'm at a loss about what to do without knowing about the day."

"There has been talk, even on the back streets. On the way back from the falconry hunt in Zoshigaya, the shogun decided to stop and enjoy a cup of medicinal tea in the newly built Takada Palace at the Otsuka Medicinal Herb Garden."

"Which means?"

"You've probably heard the gossip. Touge Soujuken, the herbalist in charge of the garden, has a daughter Sayo. She is a woman with beauty unrivaled in the prefecture."

"In that case, the shogun is smitten, too."

"What?! What are you saying?"

"Well, thank you very much. From what you've said, I now understand the crux of this matter. I'm also aware of Sayo's beauty. She is in no way an ordinary woman. For better or worse, I will aim for success even if I pay with my life," said Heiji whose youthful face glowed with inspiration. His heart pounded like he had forgotten the difference in their ranks.

"The falconry hunt is scheduled for the day after tomorrow. I don't intend to make any mistakes. I have my own strategy. If you're not careful, this may become a duel of achievements," said Officer Miyori.

"All right."

They exchanged glances and smiles of satisfaction. The police sergeant and the detective were as different as heaven and earth, but the two shared the spirit of a master.

2

THE OTSUKA MEDICINAL HERB GARDEN, also known as Takada Gardens, was on the grounds of what is now the Gokoku-ji Temple in Otowa. Beginning with the famous Physician Shrine and the Divine Farmer Shrine on fifteen acres, a magnificent building called Takada Palace was also provided to accommodate visits by the shogun.

The shrine was an imposing structure with a gabled cypress roof and rusted bronze tiles. The aroma from several hundreds of thousands of medicinal and sacred herbs was the sweet scent blanketing the surrounding ten-block radius in Otowa. The shogunate's medicinal garden had immense authority and had never been the sort of place a detective or a police officer could approach.

Zenigata Heiji rushed from Sergeant Sasano's residence and soon arrived in Otsuka. He stuck close to the fence charged with a medicinal odor. A place is only a place, but he lacked a plan to get inside.

For half the day, Heiji looked like a bungling prowler and ran out of patience around noon.

"Dammit."

He clicked his tongue as he pulled out a single Ming Dynasty *zenigata* brass coin from his sleeve and placed it in the palm of his hand. He flipped the coin using the nail of his middle finger and the pad of his thumb. The coin rang out as it flew up two or three feet into the air. When the coin dropped back down to his palm, he divined his fortune.

"Okay, it says to go home."

He dropped the coin back into his sleeve and walked away from the fence and straight to Otowa Boulevard. This coin was one reason for his nickname Zenigata Heiji. The other was a mysterious skill he possessed. When engaged in a difficult arrest, he'd jump back five feet, whip out the Chinese-made coin from his belly band, and launch it at the villain's face. Because the coin was thin and small, but weighty, even if thrown carelessly, the thief or thug flinched giving Heiji the opportunity to foil and arrest him. Thus, despite his youth, Zenigata Heiji was feared like a demon in the criminal world.

Because Heiji gave up on this mission, the secrets beyond the garden fence would not be easily revealed. In a fit of anger, he walked all the way to 9-chome of Otowa Boulevard when he stopped in his tracks. At the top of a hill called Mejirozaka, an indigo shop curtain hung motionless. Recently, the name of the cosmetics shop called Karahana-ya echoed throughout Edo. For some unknown reason, he read the signboards with gilt lettering placed out front. One board read *Water from the Garden's sponge cucumbers*. Another read *Face powders. Secret process of the southern barbarians*. And another one read *Variety of Secret Medicines Formulated by Touge*.

"This is it."

Without thinking, Heiji lowered his head to meditate.

3

"Is Shizu here?"

"Oh, hello Captain."

Heiji peeked into one of the roadside teahouses along the road going east and west in Ryogoku and said, "Oh, you're as beautiful as always. It's a crime, Shizu."

"Captain, if you keep talking like that, I will become disagreeable."

"No, I'm sorry. Don't run away. Today, I have an important favor to ask of you. Oshi-chan, have you shopped at the popular shop Karahana-ya in Otowa?"

"No. All of my friends have shopped there, but I haven't been there yet."

"I see. With looks like yours, you don't need face powders imported from the southern barbarians or water made from cucumber sponges."

"Oh, Captain."

Of course, her looks were breathtaking. She was no more than seventeen or eighteen years old. Her oval face with its fresh complexion was enchanting. The red apron she wore completely covered her cotton kimono with hanging sleeves. Despite the nature of her job, she was judged to be an honest young woman with the purity of a fruit plucked off a branch.

"The truth is... this is a difficult request. Shizu, can you take the rest of the day off and go shopping with me at Karahana-ya?

"Yes, yes, I'll go with you."

Her reply held no trace of ill feelings.

"I thank you. So before you change your mind..."

The detective and the teashop girl made an exceptionally attractive couple. For some time, the two seemed to have inklings of an awakening love in their hearts. This rumor spread swiftly.

The couple rode palanquins from Ryogoku to Kobinata. Then, Shizu walked by herself the short distance to the entrance of Karahana-ya. It was nearing six in the evening when she arrived. Shizu wore her hair in the style of a respectable young lady. From a distance at the foot of Dainichzaka hill, Zenigata Heiji watched her checkered yellow, silk-lined kimono tied with an *obi* sash with a mottled scarlet pattern disappear behind the shop curtain of Karahana-ya. At that instant, he felt like everything went black before his eyes. He had no reason to be suspicious of Karahana-ya. Perhaps, his professional sixth sense was triggered. Nonetheless, a hunch flashed through his mind that Shizu might become a sacrificial lamb.

"May I please have sponge cucumber water?"

Shizu had no trouble with her task. She had already closed her white parasol with ease and taken a seat beside the door.

"Ah, welcome. We have water from cucumbers picked this year. Tokudon, bring over a jar for the young lady."

Despite being a shop where beautiful customers were a common sight, excitement swelled. Two or three sales clerks scurried over to her from the left and the right, like iron shards drawn to a magnet.

"And...I would also like to purchase face powder."

"Yes. Yes."

"And rouge too."

Shizu was told the bundle would be large, as she quickly scanned the shop. The building was new and had an up-to-date look, but the powerful and strange quirkiness and gloominess of the shop weighed down on her delicate nerves.

"A cup of tea, miss?"

A young shop boy poured green tea, which seemed out of place in this shop, into a luxurious red teacup, which better suited the shop, and gently placed the cup beside Shizu.

"Thank you."

She looked like a proper young woman who may not drink tea, but having worked in a teashop, Shizu was accustomed to serving and drinking tea. She grasped the cup with her lovely fingers resembling pink coral and took two sips.

"Oh my?"

She thought the tea had a strange sweetness and a peculiar smell. Still, she daintily took a third sip.

While the clerks meticulously filled a small-mouthed, unglazed jar with sponge cucumber water and wrapped up the face powder and rouge, Shizu attempted to retrieve coins from her obi. Suddenly, her hair attractively styled in the sexless and innocent Shimada-mage style flopped forward as she was overcome by a terrifying feeling of sleepiness she had been fighting.

"Tokudon, watch outside. You, help me."

The head clerk stood to give familiar orders to initiate a mysterious task.

"This one is a treasure."

"Excellent."

The two young assistants lifted Shizu whose red skirt and white legs dangled down like she were dead.

Otowa Boulevard was empty. At the bottom of Dainichizaka, Zenigata Heiji, whose eyes glowed in the twilight darkness, suspected nothing.

4

AT THAT MOMENT, HEIJI recalled reports of frequent disappearances throughout Edo of young women described as pretty. Three vanished just this fall: Natsu, the daughter of a dealer in household goods in Shiba Isarago; En, the younger sister of a sake dealer in Shimoyatake-machi; and Kou, the daughter of a vassal in Azabukougai-cho. All were incomparable beauties. Because no notes were left behind, they seemed to have been spirited away. However, by the third day at the earliest or the seventh day at the latest, the shocking sight of a butchered corpse was discovered in a river, deep in the forest, or in a place where people often come and go.

The magistrates of Minami- and Kita-cho ordered the sergeants and officers under their commands to mobilize the detectives of Edo to find this demonic criminal, but they found nothing. Not only was the fiend unknown, no one could figure out why he targeted exceptionally beautiful women to kill. Also, each corpse had been bathed and then dumped, but clear traces of gold leaf remained all over her body.

"That's it."

As Zenigata Heiji nodded to himself, he peered through the twilight dusk, noticed the palanquin leaving the back door of Karahana-ya, and trailed it. His first suspicion was Shizu was inside.

The palanquin had no lanterns and promptly turned down a backstreet of Otowa and entered, as if swallowed, the back gate of the Otsuka Medicinal Herb Garden.

"Of course."

Heiji thought about returning to report to Sergeant Sasano and organize a raid on the garden. The insight about the garden was crucial. However, without a direct order from the advisers to the Council of Elders, the hands of a town magistrate were tied. Any delay may lead to the grave consequence of the end of Shizu's life.

"First, I must rescue Shizu."

Thinking about his actions later, this event made him reckless and may have awakened his love. Without thinking, he grabbed onto the earthen wall in the shadows of the trees and effortlessly scaled it to land in the dark garden.

He had no idea how much time passed or where they had gone. Several hundred thousand species, like poria cocos mushrooms, cinnamon, trifoliate orange, hawthorn, tetradium ruticarpum, angelica, anemarrhena, ginseng, fennel, Chinese asparagus root, mustard, *imonto, funahara*, and digitalis, grew thick together with countless medicinal herbs in the fifteen-acre garden. Heiji wandered this maze until he spotted a pinpoint of light and slipped into a pitch-black building.

Perhaps he was in the famous Takada Palace. In any case, the palatial building was the perfect place to prowl around. As he went from the hallways into rooms, storerooms, and stairs selected to avoid people and lights, in time, Heiji entered a sealed room in the attic.

Aha! he thought and searched for an exit. He wondered, What is the mechanism? The door and windows were covered on all sides by thick oak planks without even a crack for an ant to pass through.

"Hmm, I'll find her somehow."

He gathered his courage and sat with a thud. From a great hall below, light mysteriously leaked through small and large holes dotted the floor.

When he took a closer look, all of the holes were filled with glass. From this attic, he could observe the situation below. He looked and saw things like the eyes of heavenly beings, impressions of the wings of butterflies, and the stamens of peony drawn on the entire coffered ceiling of the great hall below.

5

HEIJI FIRST GLIMPSED A SCENE of an indescribably grotesque and vile idol. In front and on both sides of it, the red flames of thirteen pitch-black candles blazed.

In front of the evil idol, the grotesque offerings of a lizard's corpse, a cat's brain, and a half-dead snake were placed on a tall wooden stand. An animated naked body lay face up on a large unvarnished wood altar for sacrifice in the center of the strange offerings. Beside the body, the broad blade of a kitchen knife was plunged into the board.

"Ah!"

The shocked Heiji bit his lip. The baby on the sacrificial altar was neither crying nor screaming, but happily grinning. This was in stark contrast to the hair-raising, evil scene in the gloomy air enveloping the baby.

A ghastly chorus unlike anything he had ever heard erupted and a group of men and women entered the hall like a procession of ghosts. They wore black masks; only their eyes shined. Chanting voices from behind the masks filled the hall with dread.

Four women dressed in fiery crimson cloth appeared with a lone young woman. As he watched the young woman walking in a dreamlike state being pushed onto a pedestal without resistance, he realized the captive dressed like any girl in town was Shizu.

"Ah! At last."

Heiji was on the verge of crying out at the outrageous sight. If he tried to force his way into this secret room, he might slow them down, but they'd probably get away. He could not allow that.

The bizarre chant grew for some time. The ring of people dressed in black surrounding the evil idol and Shizu began circling.

This went on for a while. When silence returned to the hall, the human ring broke apart. While Shizu stood on the pedestal for some time, the hands of the people dressed in black applied a sticky gold leaf to the youthful skin of the seventeen-year-old virgin. Shizu did not move as she stood erect with her head tilted up slightly like a doll devoid of a soul and at their mercy.

When they finished placing gold leaf on the upper half of the virgin's body, a tall man in black, who appeared to be elderly, took off his hooded black mask and went to stand before Shizu.

"Ah!"

Heiji almost cried out again. The man had a frightening glow like a demon who slipped out of a picture of hell.

"..."

The man who removed his mask was Touge Soujuken, the caretaker of the garden. The gray-haired elderly man began to make ostentatious gestures.

Two people stepped forward to stand in front and behind her and touched their lips to the shoulders of the virgin covered in gold leaf. Five or six others draped in black took off their masks and showered the virginal body with kisses.

This blasphemous practice horrified Heiji. He wanted to act, but what could he do to preserve the purity of Shizu? What was the design of this secret room? He searched a second time, but could not find the way out.

The hall below filled with a bustling crowd. As he watched, four half-naked, beautiful women wrapped in the blazing red cloth started to dance a scandalous dance in a circle with the evil idol of the beast with a human face and the golden Shizu at the center.

Many strange scents rose from a huge incense burner in front of the evil idol. When Heiji smelled those aromas in the attic, he became drowsy.

He faded in and out of consciousness several times. When awake, he watched the gathering in the hall. When unconscious, he fell into a deep sleep and lost track of time. He could not continue this way and gathered all his strength, clenched both fists, and forced open both eyes to regain his senses, but like a drunk, he collapsed. He couldn't exert himself forever.

As fragments of the grotesque ceremony degrading the golden virgin Shizu burned Heiji's eyes and ears, everything became incoherent like an event from long ago.

6

THE NEXT DAY WOULD BE October 9, the day the third shogun Tokugawa Iemitsu would travel incognito to Zoshigaya for falconry hunting accompanied by a party of twelve vassals. Four of the twelve would be pages dressed identically to the shogun. Another four would be the falconers. The remaining four would be the guards. Traveling incognito was easily accomplished in those days. By order of Iemitsu, soldiers would be positioned close to him to obstruct any view of him. From Otowa through Kobinata and all the way to Otsuka, an unknown number of guards in the thousands would be stationed without space for an ant to crawl through.

Iemitsu was in a bad mood because of the unusually poor hunt that day. The pages were silent. When the hunt ended, the party headed to the Takada Palace in the Otsuka Medicinal Herb Garden, which was prepared to receive the party.

Touge Soujuken, a man about fifty with his hair pulled back in a knot, greeted them at the front gate of the garden. He had always been an herbalist, never a warrior, and wore ceremonial attire made of hemp cloth to escort the party to the palace.

An interior room was prepared with elegant furnishings. The pages were reserved, but the shogun had to be completely relaxed. On the bluish-green tatami with decorative *koraiberi* edging, the shogun leaned on an armrest and looked off into the distance at the sliding screen with the score of *Mogusa* written on smooth *torinoko* paper. The decorative openwork tracings of many insects in the rare foreign wood and the handles and knobs carved by masters added a touch of wonder to the room's casual air.

At that moment, a young woman pulled back the sliding partition. She entered and respectfully carried a teacup by holding it just below her eyes. She was Sayo, the daughter of Touge Soujuken. Her small sleeves were embroidered with the auspicious combination of pine, bamboo, and plum on a salmon-colored background. The elegance of her hair tied in a style popular in town was reflected in Iemitsu's eyes, who was bored with the customs of the long-time ladies of the court. She was twenty-two or -three years old, a little old, but her stunning beauty was not found in a tradesman's house or a samurai residence.

Pale and trembling, she walked two or three steps toward Iemitsu to bring the teacup.

"A cup of medicinal tea, Shogun," she said smiling without reservation and her eyes cast down. Usually, Iemitsu would never witness such forward behavior. Like a daimyo passing through the red-light district with ease, the passion of the shogun Iemitsu in falconry in Zoshigaya was natural.

"..."

Without a word, Iemitsu took the cup. The herbalist Touge Soujuken did not describe what type of medicinal tea he infused, perhaps, it refreshed the mind and purged noxious vapors. Iemitsu brought it to his lips and smelled the aroma of the expensive medicine.

7

SHUT UP IN THE attic, Heiji had no idea how many minutes, no, how many days he was unconscious. His eyes popped open to see brightness and dust on all sides. He remembered the bizarre dance and felt nauseous. He was worried about Shizu's safety and peeked through a glass hole again. The expansive hall was put in order and filled with a white light with no signs of the idol or the other cursed objects.

He remembered to continue searching for an exit; this time he found it. The walls were covered by thick oak planks. Only one spot had a railing. He instantly knew that was the exit. He tried pushing and hitting the spot for some time. Why was it springy? Suddenly it opened. Maybe, the mechanism was under the footboard beneath the door.

He leaped into a swelling white light. Unfortunately, a throng of people filled the garden, the hallways, the meeting hall, and the entryway. He would be unable to jump down from the attic with arms swinging and walk away.

"This is no good. Today is the shogun's falconry hunt."

Finally, Heiji came out of his fog and regained his memory. He intended to capture the villain with the poisoned arrow, but getting trapped in the ceiling foiled his plan.

"I've messed this up."

He stamped his foot in frustration in the attic.

More time passed. The air in the palace suddenly became tense.

He heard murmurs about the shogun's arrival spreading to all corners.

The arrival of the shogun was proof his conclusion about the falconry hunt made sense. Heiji let out a sigh of relief when those words reached him. He thought, if there's any trouble, he is on the palace grounds. In that case, there's still hope.

For quite some time, Heiji walked from roof to roof and from joist to joist, then slipped out through a panel and stepped under a detached roof. When he turned his head slightly, he saw the raised koraiberi tatami through an open sliding partition and could see comfortably seated knees covered by black *habutae* silk cloth.

"Ah! The shogun."

The moment Heiji stretched his neck he could see Sayo offering the cup of medicinal tea.

Just as Iemitsu took the tea in his hands, another motion caught Heiji's eyes. An elderly man was crouched like a shadow outside of the *shoji* screen. He wore his hair in a knot and was dressed in a patterned *arare-komon*, ceremonial kimono with his hands properly folded. He was, without a doubt, Touge Soujuken, the caretaker of the garden, who performed last night's grotesque ceremony.

When Iemitsu lifted the cup to his lips, Soujuken's lips twisted and his pupils seemed to radiate a light that passed through the shoji screen.

Ah! The tea's poisoned, Heiji thought.

The sixth sense found only in Zenigata Heiji stirred. He appraised the situation and knew the cup held in the hands of Iemitsu did not contain proper medicinal tea, which Sergeant Sasano often ordered.

Heiji was about to leap out from the canopy, but the detective had no reason to jump out in front of the shogun, so he considered shouting. But that brash spectacle from an outsider would lead to a melee, and he would recklessly expose himself to his rival and create a treacherous situation. The idea of poisoned tea was only a suspicion. It might actually be medicinal tea.

He suddenly remembered and searched his bellyband. Unfortunately, there was no coin only a few small silver nuggets and one thin gold *koban* coin. In those days, the koban was valuable, a fortune to a police detective. The day before yesterday, Sasano Shinsaburo gave him this coin. But the life of the shogun was at stake. This was no time to be cheap.

Instantly, the gold coin stood between the thumb and index finger of his right hand. He wetted its edge with spit and employed his special coin throwing skill to slice the air with the bright golden yellow koban and strike the bottom rim of the teacup in Iemitsu's hand thirty feet away. The teacup flew apart and ruined the fine floor cushion and tatami.

"..."

Iemitsu was unperturbed. He raised his head and stared in the inbound direction of the coin.

Sayo gasped. She stood, cheerily approached, and spread out her body and her embroidered sleeves at the knees of Iemitsu drenched in medicinal tea.

8

"WHAT ARE YOU DOING?" asked Iemitsu.

Sayo laid her face on her sleeve as if chasing the knees of Iemitsu who hurried to sit properly.

The next instant, she shot to her feet and cried out, "He's an impostor!"

"At last, you realized that."

"Oh, this is a shame. Who are you?"

Iemitsu outstretched his arm to seize the obi sash of the woman as she jumped back.

"I am Sergeant Sasano Shinsaburo. I borrowed the shogun's seat. We saw through this scheme hatched by your father and you. Now come along quietly," he introduced himself not in a loud voice, but in a casual tone.

"This is horrible" was heard coming from the other side of the shoji screen where Touge Soujuken sat; his eyes blazed with spite. He heard his daughter gasp followed by Sasano Shinsaburo's introduction. He was quick to his feet as his daughter Sayo bitterly said from the other side of the shoji screen, "Father, we've been discovered. Hurry, the land mines!"

"Oh! Sayo, if I must..."

As he deftly leaped off the narrow porch, Zenigata Heiji flew down from the roof.

"You bastard, where are you going?"

From the beginning, Heiji, who gained famed by nabbing criminals, left little room for him to escape. However, Soujuken was cornered and had unbelievable physical strength. Also, Heiji hadn't eaten in two days, sprained his ankle when he jumped off the roof, and his movements were limited.

"Eh! Outta my way!"

The two grappled with neither one winning nor losing. The pages were too far away when the situation abruptly changed. They were unable to help despite running at full speed.

In the meantime, Sayo groped to loosen the bindings behind her back, slipped out of Sasano's hand like an armload of thick planks, and took off like a scared rabbit. The father and daughter exchanged their final words.

"Father, I'll set off the land mines!"

"I'm counting on you, my dear. Don't let the sacrificial offering escape."

The sleeves embroidered with pine, bamboo, and plums flew deep into the inner room like a large bird.

Hearing about sacrifice shocked Heiji. If the desperate Soujuken and his daughter intended to blow up Takada Palace with land mines, the life of the pathetic Shizu would be snuffed out with ease. The body of the virgin covered with gold leaf and placed on the pedestal was surely hidden in that hall.

"Sergeant, take care of him please," said Heiji.

"Yes. I understand."

Inside, they could still hear the retreating footsteps of the running pages. Soujuken lunged ferociously at Heiji only to be knocked down to the grass. Heiji stepped back to chase down Sayo. His sprained ankle felt like it had been struck by a branding iron, but he couldn't complain now.

He entered the great hall he explored earlier. The pungent smell of gunpowder struck him. Soon the fuse of the land mines would be lit.

Overwhelmed by peril, Heiji's hair stood on end. He could not find where Shizu had been hidden.

"You're Zenigata Heiji. Well, it's too late. We will die together."

Sayo with her black hair and clothes in disarray cackled wildly while standing before a large wooden screen decorated with a stormy sea painted in gold. Her sinister eyes glowed.

"Woman, what happened to the girl?"

"I don't know."

"No, you do know. Tell me!"

"I won't tell you. I'll never tell you. You ruined everything. That girl who babbles your name when delirious will be blown to bits along with this palace. It will be wonderful. She's probably your lover. You don't know it, but I already lit the fuse. Ha, ha, ha, ha."

"No, I will save Shizu."

"Fool."

In the macabre scene, the beautiful woman flung her arms around and laughed insanely before the crest of stormy, furious deep-blue waves on the partition screen. The experienced Heiji instinctively staggered back. The pungent smell of gunpowder returned him to his senses. Sayo's eyes summoned her heart and soul and fixated on him like a venomous snake.

"You'll never know. It's already over."

"No, I know."

What was Heiji thinking as he leaped onto the fearsome Sayo's body? He grabbed her slender arms, and she stumbled back. When the partition screen toppled forward, behind it was a six-legged Chinese chest used by businesses inscribed with *Herb Garden*. He used all his strength to lift the lid and revealed the brilliantly golden, innocent virgin.

Shizu covered entirely in gold was inside and half dead. She was waiting for her destiny of being thrown away or killed.

"Ah! I'll get you out of here."

Heiji kicked back at Sayo clinging to him from behind. Dragging his aching leg, he carried the golden virgin under his arms and rushed outside. The instant he cleared the building, he heard a deafening roar that could shatter heaven and earth.

Enveloped by flames rising to the sky, Takada Palace crumbled into dust.

9

IT LATER EMERGED THAT in his former life, Touge Soujuken was an attendant to Major Counselor Suruga Tadanaga. He was fortunate to have knowledge of medicinal herbs and went to Kyoto to further study their mysteries. He concealed his identity until he rose to take charge of the Otsuka Medicinal Herb Garden.

After Tadanaga's suicide forced by his elder brother Iemitsu, Touge was said to resent Iemitsu and set up an altar in Takada Palace and recited incantations to dedicate the shrine to Satan, which was popular during medieval times. Because countless sacrificial offerings were required at that time, his plan was to have his close associates open a haberdashery called Karahana-ya on 9-chome in Otowa to ferret out the beautiful women of Edo and to kidnap the most beautiful among them for sacrifice. Over successive nights, incantations to Satan were chanted in secret to curse the shogun Iemitsu.

Nevertheless, he saw no progress. Recently, his resentment emerged in the actions of the shooting of the poisoned arrow and the offering of poisoned tea by his beautiful daughter Sayo. However, Magistrate Asakura Iwami-no-kami advised the Council of Elders to employ Sergeant Sasano Shinsaburo, who bore a resemblance to the shogun Iemitsu, in a splendid scheme to outfox Touge.

Touge Soujuken killed himself during the investigation, but his daughter Sayo was not seen again.

Soon after, as everyone knows, the Otsuka Medicinal Herb Garden was razed and, in the first year of the Tenna era (1681-1684), donated to become the site of Gokoku-ji Temple.

Zenigata Heiji simply did his job and subdued a mortal enemy who targeted the life of the shogun, but was unable to hand over the villain of the falconry hunt as he promised Sasano Shinsaburo. Given the nature of the incident, he received no public recognition. However, the name Zenigata Heiji made a deep impression in the heart of Iemitsu. Of greater importance, he captured the love of Shizu, the golden virgin. This more than satisfied young Heiji.

CHAPTER TWO

FURISODE GENTA

1

FURISODE GENTA STARTED A THEATER in Ryogoku to be the first since the dawn of the Edo shogunate to showcase acrobats. The amazing beauties with bangs and the splendid, novel performances gained popularity among the *Edokko*, the citizens of old Tokyo.

Unknowingly lured in by its good reputation, Heiji, aka Zenigata, was immersed in the atmosphere of the theater for half of a spring day. He planned to stop by a small neighborhood restaurant opening for evening drinks. It was already early evening when he reached Ryogoku Bridge.

Under the moonlight of the sixteenth evening of the month, movements about sixty feet ahead of him caught his eye. A man had hung one leg over the railing and looked about to jump into the river.

"Oh no!" he said. If he shouted as he ran the long distance, the man may decide to jump.

Heiji reflexively stuck his hand in his sleeve to retrieve a Ming dynasty coin between the index finger and thumb of his right hand, then took quick aim and flung the coin. His skill was frightening; he hit the man's side-lock as he was about to jump.

"Eeyah! What was that?"

The man pulled his leg back in from the railing and glared at Heiji like he could sink his teeth into him.

"Hey, that's dangerous. Since I'm not good at playing a *kappa* water sprite, if you jumped in, I'd have to leave you to your fate," said a smiling Heiji as he pressed his rival's sleeve. He saw an elderly man of substance

16

around fifty-six or -seven years old, but not the type who would throw himself, even mistakenly, off a bridge.

"Your action was unwarranted. Look here, is it swelling up?" softly chided the old man, who forgot all about jumping and was frequently wetting his temple with spit.

"Forgive me. If I had not acted, it would have been too late. In exchange for your life, I can bear opening a hole in your temple."

"I am a lawless man. I apologize."

The old man was not even-tempered, but the blow from the Ming dynasty coin seemed to eliminate his wish to die.

Heiji soon returned to the small restaurant in Higashi Ryogoku with the old man he discouraged from jumping in order to hear his story.

"People don't die as a joke. Tell me frankly. This is not about money or intelligence. What are you hiding? My name is Heiji, and I work for the shogun's government. You can depend on and take me into your confidence."

"What? Are you Captain Zenigata? A fine man saved me. In that case, I must tell you. Please listen to the whole story."

The old man told a strange story of this world in an honest tone.

2

"ON 4-CHOME NIHONBASHI BOULEVARD, Fukuya Zenbei opened a dry goods shop with a fifty-feet-wide facade, at the time a competitor of Echigoya (the predecessor of today's Mitsukoshi department store). Fukuya was the master of a large household with as many as eighty apprentices and shop boys. However, a series of shocking incidents began near the end of the previous month. One after another, three of his five children disappeared.

"The first time was the twenty-fifth of last month. The twenty-four-year-old eldest son vanished like smoke in broad daylight from the Nihonbashi shop. When this month came, on the fifth day, the twenty-one-year-old second son went missing at night from the Nihonbashi residence.

"That alone may be thought of as the chance of fate, but yesterday, the fifteenth, the third child, the eighteen-year-old daughter was kidnapped on the way to stay at the home of relatives.

"When we realized the children were disappearing in order of age every ten days, the incidents became impossible to think of as accidents. The master Zenbei was in agony and searched all over as if 'the power of money would put an end to this.' Strangely, the whereabouts of the three children are unknown. And no traces of their whereabouts were discovered."

Zenigata Heiji was aware of these incidents, but after hearing it again from a person involved, he sensed a serious crime behind these events.

"I was escorting the young lady, the third one, to her relatives' home, but she disappeared. I cannot face the shame of returning to Fukuya. After a full day and night, ultimately, I found no clues and was at a loss for what to do. On an impulse, I was going to drown myself."

The loyal old man finished talking, and tears poured down.

"After hearing your story, I understand, but if you died, the young woman will never see home again."

"Oh, I see."

"All right, I'll take the lead. Since no ordinary person committed those acts, although challenging, it is a worthy job. Now, can you return home looking untroubled and report back to me about the situation inside?"

"You will help me, Captain? I thank you with the strength of one thousand men."

Zenigata Heiji saved a man and jumped right into a case.

3

HEIJI HEADED TO FUKUYA to spend the day. He discovered nothing about how the three missing siblings were lured away. The limitations of the police of that day had been reached and fallen short. Also, the townspeople weren't the least bit reliable. Therefore, a case this serious was left unreported. He wanted to approach the eighty or so apprentices and the members of the family, but everyone was distraught.

Above all, the master Zenbei looked like a sick man. When he saw the well-respected police detective Heiji, he said, "Captain, please search for those three. If warranted, it wouldn't matter if it cost half the wealth of Fukuya."

He implored Heiji not to give up.

The remaining family members were a sixteen-year-old daughter Ito and a boy Eizaburo, who will be six, and his second wife of only one year, Taki. Considering the ways of the world, this stepmother Taki drew the most suspicion.

Aware of that, too, she was pitiful and nervous when she met the detective Heiji. However, Heiji did not see a monstrously evil woman.

She was about thirty-two or -three years old, a little young for Zenbei, but pretty and dignified, befitting the wife in a prosperous family. Her initial reputation was not bad among the employees.

Because all eighty or so employees could not be investigated thoroughly, Heiji relied on indisputable evidence given to him by the head clerk and concluded not one of them was suspicious.

Given these circumstances, Heiji left to brief Sergeant Sasano Shinsaburo about the case.

"Of course, that is odd. If you dive into the investigation, an unexpected important figure may emerge. You should observe them a bit longer."

Heiji was encouraged by Sasano's words.

Before a few days passed, the Fukuya family experienced a new upset. Following the previous examples, on the twenty-fifth, it was the younger daughter Ito's turn to become the fourth child to disappear.

Ito and her missing older sister Kiyo were pretty and called The Two Belles of Nihonbashi. Ito understood the terrifying danger hanging over her, and her melancholy built up day by day. Her father Zenbei was more distressed than she.

If she were out of his sight for even a moment, he'd call out, "Ito, where are you? Ito?" as he scoured the house in search of her. He was hopeless when she was not in front of him.

Fukuya Zenbei appealed, "Too many people come and go at this place that is impossible to guard. Therefore, from the evening of the twenty-fourth, Ito will stay at the dormitory in Mukojima. Captain, I'm sorry to ask you at such a busy time, but could you stay by my daughter's side on that day, the twenty-fifth. If so, I would feel more reassured than with one hundred other men by her side."

Heiji said, "My rival is not weak. I may be able to watch over and protect her. If you accept that, I will be there on that day."

Zenigata Heiji would be there, but he didn't sound confident.

4

ON THE TWENTY-FIFTH, the protection of the younger daughter Ito and the watch at the Mukojima dormitory could not be described as showy or overdone. Fifteen or sixteen strong sales clerks from the Nihonbashi store came along with five or six of Heiji's men. The addition of guards and maids at the dormitory, staff from the shop attached to Ito, and helpful neighbors brought the total to over thirty people. This crowd encircled the beautiful Ito. For the whole day, the guard would not even let water slip through.

Nothing happened during the day, but the preparations were excessive. When night came, everyone looked drawn and drained of color. Heiji was encouraged and took his post without any objection. Two men were stationed at each entrance to the dormitory. At locations considered vulnerable, a man was stationed at each storm shutter so that not even a gap existed to allow an ant to crawl through.

From early morning, Ito had been shut up in her room with her favorite maid Chiyo. Despite the importance of keeping watch, Heiji could not invade the sleeping quarters of the sixteen-year-old girl called the Belle of Nihonbashi to guard her and see her lovely sleeping face. Fortunately, the two paths to the room were blocked, and two of Heiji's trusted men kept watch on the corridors. Heiji; the head clerk Kashichi, who came from Nihonbashi; and the husband and wife caretakers of the dormitory encamped in the adjacent room and were determined to talk the night away.

"Miss, it's time for bed. Your change of clothes is here..."

They understood the situation next door from the maid's words. Not long after, they appeared to have fallen asleep amid the fear, when noises from the adjacent room ceased.

When Heiji gave the caretakers a meaningful look, the wife stood and opened a peephole in the papered sliding door. In the shadow of the dim paper-covered lampshade inside, even Heiji could see the girl's head sunk deep into the gaudy bedding.

"..."

The wife nodded, closed the sliding door, and returned to her seat.

For a while, the sounds of a small riverboat were heard passing along the opposite shore into Sanyabori canal. Finally, the Mukojima shore grew hushed as in ancient times.

About ninety minutes later, not one person inside or outside the house was sleeping. An unusual excitement amplified by each passing moment was suppressed. When morning light was seen slipping through the window, everyone had the profound feeling of having been rescued.

"Oh, thank goodness," declared the caretaker wife and slapped her forehead with the palm of her hand.

When she opened the sliding storm shutter, the spring sun filled the house with unsparing delight and hope.

Suddenly, the maid's voice from the adjacent room cried out, "Oh no! The miss is..."

When they knocked down the sliding door as they rushed into the room, Ito's bedding was empty. Her maid Chiyo seated beside it was aghast and unable to speak.

Heiji leaped at the bedding and stuck his hand inside. Body heat remained. If she had been kidnapped, she wasn't too far away.

"Nobody leaves this dorm. Reinforce each post. If any stranger rushes out, whistle."

Heiji's commands echoed in the morning air from the edge of the veranda where he stood.

For half the day, the dormitory boiled over with panic. Tatami mats were raised, sliding doors and screens removed, and attics entered in searches that would not overlook a single mouse. The scoundrel was foolish enough to think Ito, who sparkled, would not be seen if hidden in a dark place.

Needless to say, the master Zenbeei was in anguish and stepmother Taki was in shock over the fourth kidnapping of their daughter. Zenigata Heiji felt disgraced.

Only a man with an abundance of pride would be too ashamed and unable to face Zenbei and his wife. As he plodded along the bank to return to the main residence in Tokyo, a hand was gently placed on Heiji's shoulder from behind.

"Well, you must feel awful?"

"Huh?"

When Heiji turned around, he faced a forty-year-old man, a man of ability, called Ishihara Risuke from the same station. Naturally, he was Heiji's rival.

"I heard you started working on this Fukuya case, but it'd be better if you quit."

"What do you mean?"

"If it's those kidnappings, I've already made an arrest. You look totally clueless, and I don't want to humiliate you."

"What?!"

After those scathing words, Risuke continued on to Mukojima without looking back.

5

FOUR OF THE FIVE SIBLINGS had been kidnapped on days ending in five. This Fukuya case created a stir throughout Edo. Within the day, newspapers printed with tile blocks came out and were being hawked on every corner. Zenigata Heiji stayed awake and on guard but was outwitted. The value in that was the fascination of the Edokko in him.

Sergeant Sasano Shinsaburo could not leave matters as is. Zenigata Heiji was his favorite and he summoned Heiji in his official capacity, but a scowl accidentally slipped.

"Heiji, what is going on with this case? It wasn't a good fit for you."

"Yes, I truly have no excuse. I made a huge blunder by believing, at best, it was a mundane scheme of the stepmother."

"So you are saying the kidnapping was not committed by the stepmother Taki. Did you expect that to be certain?"

Sasano Shinsaburo looked a little amazed.

"I wouldn't say certain, but that masterful performance could not have been accomplished by a single woman. I can't believe the stepmother Taki is that evil."

"Well, Heiji, in time, will you be able to produce a description of the criminal?"

"Yessir."

The sergeant was a perceptive man, and Heiji said no more.

"Heiji, the truth is today Ishihara Risuke arrested the stepmother Taki."

"Ah, he actually did that."

"You knew about this?"

"No, I don't know what criminal act she committed. Because of his appalling words to me earlier, Risuke wouldn't hesitate to go that far to prevent not being outsmarted by me."

"So that's it," said Sasano without hinting whose side he was on.

"In that case, I will make a last-ditch effort. Please give me two or three days."

"I'll wait, but the next day ending in five is coming. Solving this case will become nearly impossible after all five siblings have been taken."

"Yessir."

A dejected Heiji disappeared from Sasano Shinsaburo's sight.

Filled with regret, he went from Hatchobori to Okawabata on the late spring evening and looked like he wanted to cry.

At least, if someone said, "Give us money to get your children back," Heiji would know the reason. Even if blood is not shed and money is not wanted, what on Earth was the aim of this brutality? He had no idea.

6

"OH, SIR, IT'S BEEN A WHILE. What have you been up to?" asked Heiji.

"Good morning Captain. I've been keeping busy with odd jobs at the Nihonbashi store. However, it's very busy at the Mukojima dormitory today, and I was asked to come here."

"I hope you no longer feel like dying."

"Yes, yes, well, thank you so much for your help at that trying time," said the old man, who was hit by the coin thrown by Heiji the other day to keep him from drowning.

"Will you be here until evening?"

"Yes, I intend to be."

"Well, I have a favor to ask of you. Will you accept it?"

"Captain, whatever you ask, I will accept and even risk my life."

"It's not that dangerous, but no one in this dormitory is as reliable as you. First of all, your willingness to die means your honesty is certain. You may play the critical role. Let me explain."

Heiji brought his mouth close to the old man's ear to whisper.

"Yes, yes, of course."

"Do you understand? Make sure no one learns of this."

"Yes, yes."

The old man was easily recruited. They finished their preparations during the morning without raising suspicions.

The last treasure of Fukuya Zenbei, his fifth child Eizaburo, was the target. Therefore, from the morning of the fifth, Heiji entered the Mukojima dorm to make elaborate preparations like the battle preparations of Hachimon Tonkou.

The inability of the villain to enter from the entrances or the storm shutters was well understood. Tonight, the guards outside were withdrawn. Close to thirty people were gathered inside the house.

The dormitory did not have a large room. Therefore, the partitions between the inner eight-tatami room and two six-tatami rooms were removed. The target Eizaburo was placed inside. Around him were the full army numbering more than thirty consisting of Heiji's men, the Fukuya's shop workers, head clerks, and neighbors. The crowd formed two close circles, two people deep, to surround him.

Although it was a warm time of the year, the cold chill of dawn was taken into account, and two charcoal slabs were placed in a large brazier. Tobacco trays, tea, and candy were provided to leave no room to step. There were also four large candles with the light of one hundred candles. Two were on the left and right of Eizaburo and protected by the maid Chiyo. The other two were at the entrance to the room and guarded by a well-known neighborhood girl.

Heiji and the master Zenbei sat opposite each other and had not stood since the evening began but chatted from time to time. Because the stepmother Taki had been arrested, Zenbei looked pitiful, like his spirit had been broken, and seemed to suddenly age ten years. Others saw an inconsolable man.

If the all-night vigil were a wake, the departed would be remembered in stories, but there was no talk of the unearthly because a living person had to be protected from an attack by a mysterious supernatural scoundrel. Four times, a child was kidnapped in a different way. What technique would be used tonight? While these thoughts crossed their minds, the chill grew.

"Captain, are you all right?" Zenbei repeated this question a number of times over a short period.

"I can't say. Anyway, I will try to do what I can."

Heiji's answer was as good as a stamp from his seal.

7

MIDNIGHT CAME.

The anxiety and tension deepened. All those present looked like they wanted to flee. Would there be a fantastic event like an explosion? If not and they did not shout with all their might, all thirty plus people may go mad.

Among them, the pretty maid Chiyo noiselessly stood. As they wondered what was she doing, she carried brass scissors for trimming the accumulated wick of the candles and held them above a candlestick. Her sleeve brushed against and toppled over one of the candlesticks.

She snatched back her hand and the candlestick behind her overturned.

Before she could say, "Ah!" the other two candlesticks being guarded by the neighborhood girl were knocked over and the room went black.

"Eeyah!"

"Help!"

The cries were accompanied by the thudding sound of someone dropping down onto the floor. Above the din, the lone, cool voice of Zenigata Heiji shouted, "Light. Light. Bring light from the kitchen."

In the confusion, those alert to their surroundings should have rushed to the kitchen and returned with paper-covered lamps and handheld candlesticks. The cooks and the neighborhood wives in the kitchen all flinched in the midst of chaos and could not rise to act during the emergency.

"Hurry, bring light. I'll grab the young master."

After Heiji's voice was heard a second time, a couple of his men dashed out and headed to the kitchen. When they returned carrying lanterns and candlesticks, the sight in the room was....

Writhing people were scattered around the room. Utensils were strewn around leaving no place to step.

More surprising, Zenigata Heiji thought he was clutching the hem of Eizaburo's kimono. His hand gripped something that was not Eizaburo's hem but the hem of the kimono of Chiyo, who knocked over the first candle stand. Also, he clutched the glossy crimson hem while lying on his stomach as if swimming.

"Oh!"

"I don't see the young master."

"Eiza is gone!"

Of course, only a cold seating cushion where Eizaburo sat lay in the center of the room. The child had vanished.

The thirty powerless protectors were speechless for a time. The master Zenbei looked around again and again. When he realized his last beloved child had been taken, he lost all hope.

The maid Chiyo desperately freed her hem from Heiji's grip and turned to say, "It's over…"

Was she flush with victory or filled with anger? Heiji was stumped.

He thought this beautiful maid was peculiar. Because Heiji had grabbed her hem and pulled, at least, he knew Eizaburo was not hidden there.

The entire residence was searched like a major cleaning, but Heiji unraveled nothing. He jumped up and rushed out of the entrance of the dormitory to the Mukojima levee.

8

"SIR."

"Oh, Captain."

"Did you see anything?"

"Like you said, a black figure flew out of the skylight."

"Which way did he go?"

"He was carrying something, but in this darkness, I don't know what. He jumped from the roof and grabbed onto a branch of the cherry blossom tree, then he expertly crawled up the levee."

"What do you mean by expertly?"

"I tried to chase him, but he was too fast for an old man like me. I think he slid down to the levee to board a readied skiff. This time, an unskilled person rowed."

"Of course."

At another location in the shadow of the levee, the old man and Zenigata Heiji talked secretly amid the turmoil in the dormitory.

Heiji stationed the old man on the levee to keep an eye on the roof because his eyesight was keen, although he could do nothing about a fleeing villain. Whatever Heiji was thinking, he betrayed no regret but thought for a while with arms folded.

"Excuse me, Captain?"

"Shh," Heiji hushed the old man who tried to speak and hid in the shadow of an old sakura tree.

A human shadow slipped unnoticed out of the kitchen of the dormitory and approached the tree concealing the pair.

"Stop!"

"Ah!"

Heiji's hand seized her collar.

"Thought you were gonna get away. Come here."

When Heiji dragged her toward the fire, it was unmistakably the maid Chiyo.

When she was returned to the dormitory still gripped by the neck, the master Zenbei regained a little energy, but still lacked the strength to speak when confronted with this shock.

"Did she commit this crime?" asked the flustered head clerk.

Heiji said, "That's a good guess. The scoundrel got away, but his accomplice was seized. Please look at her."

The maid Chiyo he pushed forward did not seem dispirited. A sneer rose between her beautiful cheeks.

"Captain, how did the villain escape?"

While glancing back at the people crowding around him, Heiji stepped up into the alcove and into the opening in the frame between the alcove and the floor. He put one hand on the horizontal beam and pushed on the ceiling panel of the alcove. As he suspected, the ceiling panel easily opened into two panels and to blackness. When he looked down, he could see dust that appeared to have trickled from the ceiling and settled onto the flower vase in the alcove.

"Of course. The candlesticks were knocked over, and the young master was snatched. Here is where he escaped. He has knowledge of martial arts and if his body weight is light, it would not have been impossible."

What he said was not wrong, but the villain did not drop down from above and knock down Chiyo with the candle stand. He snatched the child and fled from here. From the evening, he mixed in with the group and, inexplicably, attracted no attention.

Someone asked, "Was the younger daughter kidnapped in the same way?"

"No, that was probably different. We can find out by questioning this girl. Perhaps the younger daughter was taken during the evening. This girl was one person who played two roles in the room with the daughter. There are other differences. In contrast to tonight, that night was quiet and walking above the ceiling would have been noticed. Someone certainly stayed under the floor until dawn. Maid, isn't that so?"

When questioned by Heiji, Chiyo only nodded and smiled a curiously meaningful cold smile.

One of Heiji's men said, "Captain, we must force this young woman to reveal where her accomplice is, and whether the five children are alive or dead."

The master and the head clerk, who regained their senses, heard that and were revived.

"Well, Chiyo, you've heard everything, what do you think?" asked Heiji while scrutinizing the face of the maid being seized by his men.

Chiyo said nothing. An idea seemed to cross her mind, and she raised her narrow shoulders without moving an eyebrow.

"It won't be easy getting her to talk. I have an idea about the identity of her accomplice."

"What?"

"Her accomplice was the other young woman beside the candle stand. The one with the face of a neighbor was actually a man."

More surprised than the master, the head clerk, and Heiji's men was the smug Chiyo whose earlier composure vanished.

9

THE FOLLOWING MORNING, the moment the wooden door of the exhibition theater in Ryogoku opened, the acrobatic theater of Furisode Genta was surrounded on all sides by Zenigata Heiji's men. In the absence of solid proof about kidnapping, the sergeant did not make an appearance. Zenigata Heiji with his metal truncheon intended to make an arrest and make the culprit talk to get proof. First of all, this was probably a swipe at Ishihara Risuke who arrested the stepmother. However, in those days, arrests of this type were not uncommon.

Heiji came with few men, but they had the skills of mighty warriors.

"Genta, you're under arrest."

"Surrender."

At the same time, the door opened, and police flooded in with the customers and rushed to the dressing room to surround Genta.

Furisode Genta was there dressed in a gaudy, long-sleeved stage kimono and light yellowish green, silk damask *hakama* trousers. However, when he heard "You're under arrest," he snatched a small blade placed beside him and ran to the stage and jumped around like a monkey between the trapezes, the ropes, and the wooden racks. The guests who entered and filled about half of the dirt floor were frightened by the violent arrest.

First, there was confusion, then chaos began. As the crowd jostled each other, some flew out the door and others crumpled to the floor all while shouting and crying.

"Furisode Genta, surrender. We know you kidnapped the five Fukuya siblings. You won't get away. Better than adding to these rash crimes, hand me the rope and tell me where they are."

Zenigata Heiji stood erect on the dirt floor and looked up as he spoke his echoing commands.

"Oh, Zenigata Heiji? Even a police detective like you will understand this story. So listen to me now!"

"What?"

Furisode Genta rolled up his large red patterned sleeves and took a blade in his fist. He looked down at Heiji from the top of a paper lantern hung on a pole more than three times his height.

The charming forelock of the entertainer stood up. He was probably already twenty-two or -three. He had a frightening charm, a solid jaw, large eyes, plump chin, and a figure that seemed delicate. Heiji couldn't believe he was older than seventeen or eighteen no matter how he looked at him.

"I have a grudge against that Fukuya family that can't be satisfied even if I were reborn seven times."

"..."

Seeing the ferocity of his attitude, the audience, the police, and the troupe members listened in silence.

"To tell every detail would take forever. I was ruined because of Fukuya. If I said I am a son of the house of Fukuya, even you may understand. Our branch family was set up in business by Zenbei, who rose from being the head clerk of the main family of the Fukuya that exclusively sold dry goods to the shogunate and fabrics to Western armies. Zenbei made groundless accusations about my family like slandering of the shogunate, accepting the battle flags of the rebel Christian Amakusa, or audaciously indulging in luxuries above our positions. As a result, my father was banished to a remote island and my mother fell ill and died. My family was ruined. Could you live without holding a grudge in this wretched situation caused by the main Fukuya family?"

"..."

"Finally, I chose life and fled to Nagasaki. I learned acrobatics from a foreigner, joined the troupe, and came to Edo. Zenbei's star was rising. I thought what could be more sinister than kidnapping the children one by one and bring more suffering than the death of that mangy dog. Hey, Heiji, if you were me, would you just stand by and gaze at the prosperity of your enemy?"

His beautiful face glowed with excitement. His eyes burned like fire.

10

"NO, THE CRIME MAY BE Zenbei's, but the children know nothing. Isn't that an indefensible act? Be quiet, hand over the rope, and tell me where the children are."

Heiji did not retreat.

"I'll tell you, but if I tell you, you can't rescue all five."

"What are you saying?"

"Right now the five are in a tool room. If I cut this thick rope and drop it, they will be crushed by a huge boulder, turned into fish guts, and die."

"What?!"

"Ha, ha, ha. Surprised, Heiji? I carefully considered remote possibilities and prepared. Until now, the five brothers and sisters were scattered here and there, but last night I brought all of them here and locked them in a cage previously used for a bear. A boulder weighing more than eight hundred pounds hangs from the ceiling of the cage. If I cut here, your wait won't be long. Stay there! Don't move. If you move clumsily, you'll see me cut right here."

While waving about the stage prop fitted with a real blade, he stared at the thick rope running at an incline across the crossbeam and hanging down. The uncommonly pretty man wearing large red sleeves was immersed in the pleasure of his revenge. His gleaming eyes made a ghastly sight.

"Wait! Wait, Genta. If you cut the rope and kill the children, your wife Chiyo will be executed for the crime of killing her master."

"Huh?"

At last, Heiji found Genta's weakness.

"Bring the woman here," Heiji yelled toward the door.

"Okay."

Chiyo, bound hand and foot, was led in. Without thinking, she nodded when she saw her husband Genta and said, "Oh, my dear."

Her hardened face softened and blood tinted her pretty cheeks.

"Chiyo."

"Don't worry about me. Cut the rope and end this. I want to see weeds grow on the roof of Fukuya from the crucifixion cross."

She was probably a woman with a strong spirit. Her beauty was extraordinary, but her words made grown men tremble with fear.

Heiji played his trump card.

"Wait. Wait. I have one more thing to tell you. The landlord Zenbei was overcome with grief over the kidnapping of his fifth child and died this morning."

"What?"

"That should end your vengeance. The five children are not to blame. This was unexpected and my fault. Forgive me."

"..."

"Isn't your revenge too extreme? Your wife's life will be traded for the lives of the children. When I untie this rope, you will come down."

Heiji began to untie the rope binding Chiyo. The husband in red sleeves and the wife freed from the vital knot, looking up and looking down, exchanged poignant glances.

"HEIJI, DID THOSE SERIOUS criminals escape?"

"Well, yes, they did."

Looking a little disgusted, Sergeant Sasano Shinsaburo said, "Wasn't untying Chiyo's rope and allowing her to escape with Genta a bit much?"

"I am so ashamed, sir."

Heiji shrunk like a naughty child before the young sergeant.

"Very well. Considering five lives were saved, this time only, you should placate Magistrate Asakura Iwami-no-kami-sama. Please do so later."

"Yessir, thank you."

"There are problems with your hobby, too. Ha, ha, ha."

Heiji kneeled to the smiling Shinsabura and then rushed out to the streets of Hatchobori. Cold sweat stuck to his collar.

Heiji had failed. The name Heiji of No Achievements would probably become better known thanks to this case.

The whereabouts of Furisode Genta and his wife Chiyo were still unknown. Ishihara Risuke withdrew for a while and shut himself away.

Left unsaid was the selection of days ending in five to kidnap the five siblings. Genta's father was banished on the fifth, and his mother died on the fifteenth.

CHAPTER THREE

CONFESSIONS OF THE GREAT ROBBERIES

1

A MYSTERIOUS THIEF RAVAGED EDO like a swift wind stealing objects in a way that should be beyond human ability to steal, and in less than three days, returning those objects to their owners.

"Heiji, a strict order came from Magistrate Asakura Iwami-no-kami-sama. Recently, the thief running riot about town steals an article and then returns it. Therefore, a crime may not have been committed. However, his actions show contempt for the authority of the shogun. The magistrate did not say by tomorrow, but the order is to arrest him by whatever means."

While his status differed from that of Sergeant Sasano Shinsaburo, the favorite of the magistrate of Minami-cho, Shinsaburo openly confided in this master of arrests Zenigata Heiji, who he thought of as kin.

Heiji said, "I see. I have been thinking about this, too. First of all, I don't like this method of stealing something only to return it. It's like a strange love letter or stealing from the poor. Stealing for food, while evil, is also pitiful. If returning the stolen object the next day is not the act of a man who steals as a hobby, I'm sure the intent is to mock us. If this thief isn't arrested, I will no longer be able to face the world."

Heiji was not his usual levelheaded self. He tapped his knees with clenched fists and sidled over to the door threshold on the veranda side.

Shinsaburo said, "If you feel that way, an arrest may not be far off, but few clues have been found."

"I'm ashamed to say there are no leads."

"In fact, the thief may be a woman."

"That is not certain. The person returning the stolen objects was a courtesan endowed with eye-opening beauty. If she's also the thief, her performance is superb."

"By that you mean?"

"Keys and locks were released effortlessly. Fences nine or twelve feet high were scaled, and the horizontal beam along the wall was stepped on to slip into the parlor. This performance would be impossible for a woman or a child."

"Hmmm."

Sasano Shinsaburo, Zenigata Heiji, and people of that day had great difficulty dealing with the man called the Phantom Thief Kazetaro, who casually appeared and disappeared, a vagrant who moved through the world like the wind.

"There is only one way to catch this thief," said Heiji.

"How?" asked Shinsaburo.

"The plan must be precise. Please wait a few days."

"Heiji, you are an unexpected scholar," laughed Shinsaburo.

"Yes."

The handsome and imposing Heiji did not raise his head to Sasano Shinsaburo.

2

"CAPTAIN."

"What is it Garappachi? Quiet down."

"I'm sorry. A report, a report has been communicated."

"Stop putting on airs. What is it?"

The serene Heiji looked up at his sidekick Garappachi.

"Last night, Kazetaro struck again."

"Where?"

"Ryukoji Temple in Asakusa."

"What was stolen?"

"A four-inch golden Buddha statue of *Dainichi Nyorai* from inside the miniature shrine in the main temple."

"This guy is damned."

"Captain, I didn't steal nothing."

"That's true, you have no reason to steal. Lead the way."

"I feel so much better with you coming along, Captain. This way."

"Stop fooling around."

Guided by the clownish Garappachi, who wore his lined kimono with no undergarments, hid his truncheon near his breast, and wore slip-on sandals, Zenigata Heiji soon arrived at the Ryukoji Temple in Asakusa.

The profit-minded head priest told them that the four-inch-tall, pure gold Dainichi Nyorai was a wooden *Tainai Hodoke* (a Buddha inside another Buddha) statue of the sect founder enshrined in the inner sanctum of the temple and placed in a separate miniature shrine. He had expected this to enliven the interior of the temple. However, last night, the Phantom Thief Kazetaro stole the statue.

To Kazetaro, keys and locks were no problem.

Heiji listened to the head priest grouse, repeating the same complaint over and over. He finished his investigation and search but found nothing. Unperturbed, Heiji went out to the garden where he came across a temple worker who lectured about the garden plants for half the day. Next, Heiji entered the main temple to examine the carvings, tablets, and paintings befitting a temple but did not see a miniature shrine when he turned his head to look.

"Captain, please take this task to heart and search with all your might. If that golden Buddha is gone forever... I don't have to tell you, but this temple will have no excuse for its supporters. If I must be expelled and the temple surrendered, this head priest will wither away."

"I understand. More than that, what kinds of people come and go at this temple? Each one will be watched," said Heiji.

"What?" asked Garappachi.

"If this is the work of Kazetaro, he will return. What kind of man returns what he stole? That is what I want to know."

"Naturally. Only the captain thinks like that. The punk who comes back will be the thief."

"Perhaps."

"Okay, I'll do it and not even miss a parade of ants."

Garappachi popped both eyes wide open to watch, but not one suspicious person came or went.

One day passed without incident. But when the grounds were carefully searched, an offering wrapped in paper was found beside the temple's money offering box. While not suspecting a thing, it was opened. Inside was the brilliant, four-inch, golden Tainai Hodoke — the Dainichi Nyorai.

"Ah!"

"He came during the hours you were waiting."

Zenigata Heiji was dumbfounded. Of the many men and women who visited the temple beginning in the morning, he had absolutely no idea which one was the Phantom Thief Kazetaro.

3

THE FOLLOWING NIGHT, someone attacked the pawnshop of Kasusaya Jubei in Hongo Haruki-cho by unlocking multiple locks or opening the closed front door, and then climbing over the shop grating, and crossing above the shop boys' heads into an inner room. A lock was cleanly opened, and a total of three hundred ryo in gold coins was taken from inside a cabinet placed at Jubei's bedside. And twelve rectangular rice cakes were carried off.

In those days, three hundred ryo was so large it could aptly be called a fortune. An alarmed Kasusaya Jubei filed a complaint.

"If this is the work of Kazetaro, then the items will be returned within two or three days. During that time, may I intrude on your business and work at the counter?" asked Heiji.

"What? I'm not asking you to do that. However, for the first time, after an attack by a thief, the shop workers will not be afraid."

Jubei excitedly accepted. As a precaution, Zenigata Heiji ordered Garappachi to watch the back streets and would fly out of the shop, if signaled by him. Heiji sat at the counter of Kasusaya to keep an eye on the customers.

The customers came as usual, but not one looked like a possible Kazetaro. At the height of the evening rush, a wretched state had been reached, when a young, pretty woman sat down in front of the floor lattice.

"I forgot to bring my notebook. Please let me leave this here while I go and fetch it."

She spoke like she was talking to herself and quickly passed through the shop curtain. She didn't hear the head clerk say, "Oh, leaving it there is a problem."

The young woman heard the clerk's caution behind her but dashed outside. She never returned.

"Now, that's suspicious. Of course, the young woman who brought that package is probably Kazetaro."

Zenigata Heiji was confused, but he finally realized what happened. When he opened the package left by the woman, inside was the three hundred ryo of gold coins and the rice cakes with an uncut seal. They were exactly as they had been when stolen.

"Ah!"

The surprises piled up. Heiji knew the beautiful young woman was an accomplice of the Phantom Thief Kazetaro.

4

THREE DAYS LATER, a thief snuck into the residence of a famous tea master Shigeno Yuhaku and stole a well-known teacup received as a gift from a past daimyo. Although called a well-known object, his ancestor received this treasure with history from Hotaiko for meritorious service in the invasion of Korea. This rare and famous object in the world was resented by Date Masamune, who had petitioned for half the province of Iwashiro as compensation, which in the end, was not transferred.

This robbery was achieved only by tying a rope to the neck of Shigeno Yuhaku. The only reliable element was the return of the article within three days if stolen by the Phantom Thief Kazetaro, who created the recent sensation throughout the prefecture. While waiting in vain for two days, this hope gave solace to the disheartened Yuhaku.

Today was the third day, and he could no longer bear it. Did Kazetaro treasure the famous teacup, too? Three days had passed, but the cup had not been given back. Yuhaku felt like he was at the point of no return. He lost his usual calm and paced back and forth hundreds of times between the inner room and the gate.

Zenigata Heiji was on hand for three days, but it was in vain. Fully aware of Kazetaro's trick, no scent remained to be smelled after the thief walked through like the wind. As was his custom, Heiji lay in wait for the thief to return with the article in order to catch and tie him up.

If Kazetaro entered through this gate, even if he altered his appearance, he would not escape Heiji's policeman's rope. Heiji's futile wait ended a little after noontime. With no news, he believed if the teacup were not returned, Shigeno Yuhaku would feel more dead than alive.

Sometime after two but close to four o'clock, a figure unexpectedly appeared at the kitchen door.

"That's it!" said Heiji and went out to see. The caller was the familiar boy from next door. Kazetaro, the thief who seemed to materialize from thin air, could not be this small acquaintance.

"Auntie, the lady said to tell you these are a small gift, and to please let everyone enjoy them," the boy passed on the message and handed over a porcelain bowl of *manju* buns filled with bean paste to Yuhaku's wife.

"Thank you very much," she said.

She took them and obviously wondered who sent this snack. She glanced down and saw the bowl holding the manju was the famous teacup stolen three days earlier.

"Ah! How?"

Yuhaku, who happened to come by, tossed out the manju and scrutinized the bowl from right to left like he was hugging the teacup. He examined the teacup without overlooking the faintest scratch struck by the feather of a cormorant.

"Boy, wait a moment."

Heiji jumped at the neighbor's child and in a grave tone said, "Be a good boy and tell me where the manju came from."

"I didn't do nothing. Let me go, please."

Clearly afraid, he began to cry.

As Yuhaku's wife and the boy's father from next door came to comfort him, the boy told them a pretty young woman asked him to do this favor in the alley outside. However, the child could say nothing else about her age or looks.

When Kazetaro's skilled, detailed, and nearly miraculous trick was observed, it was not the work of two or three people. They concluded it was the work of a single person possessing an unusual mind and ability. The pretty, young woman, who returned the stolen articles, must be the Phantom Thief Kazetaro.

But what were the reasons for the thefts, and why were the stolen objects returned? When the returned gold coins and teacup were examined, they were, without a doubt, the true articles in their original conditions. There wasn't the slightest trace of substitution with fakes. The thief's objective was not found in this habit of going to so much trouble to steal and not even keeping the most worthless coin.

The rumor spread throughout Edo within the day that the Phantom Thief Kazetaro might be a pretty, young woman.

5

"HEIJI, KAZETARO'S STRUCK AGAIN."

"What? Where did she strike this time?"

Summoned by Sergeant Sasano, Heiji looked down in shame. Ever since the Phantom Thief Kazetaro began rampaging through Edo about three months ago, a police detective named Enaka has been doing his best to compete in capturing the thief but had failed. Zenigata Heiji, famous for his ability to capture criminals, felt so ashamed, he would jump in a hole if one were handy.

"This one is a little puzzling."

"What do you mean?"

"Lord Akai Samon lives in a mansion in Kobinata and has a pedigree prominent even among vassals worth twenty-eight hundred *koku*. You've probably heard of him."

"The lord is a fine man around forty years old and has the favor of the shogun."

"Now to the specifics of this case. The truth is Kazetaro entered the residence of Lord Akai Samon."

"What?!"

"This time he stole two chests, each filled with one thousand ryo, passed to him by the commissioner of finance by order of the shogun."

"This is serious."

This surprised Heiji. Two chests containing two thousand ryo in today's money market are worth about four million yen. The amount of four million yen is huge when calculated relative to prices.

A chest filled with one thousand ryo is not an ordinary article. The shogun Iemitsu has unusual faith in Saint Kuya and contributed two thousand ryo to build an Ichiu temple in Rakuhoku for the saint. However, according to what became public, some procedure was problematic and involved the secret opinions held by the commissioner of finance. Akai Samon from a clan prestigious even among the Ansho vassals was appointed by written request of the shogun to be the envoy to deliver the grand sum of two thousand ryo to Shogun Iemitsu.

Akai Samon was to depart on the first day of the following month. For the next seven or eight days, the letter bearing the shogun's signature and the two thousand ryo decorated an inner room and were protected as during an all-night watch. Nonetheless, there was a gap somewhere and within the night the two chests vanished like smoke.

The fortune within the misfortune was the shogun's letter was untouched. Akai Samon was in need of money and raised the huge sum of two thousand ryo by borrowing from eight parties. If he couldn't raise the money by the date of his departure, Akai Samon would have to apologize even if it meant harakiri. Through some scheme, he consulted with his good friend Sasano Shinsaburo. The business of a town police sergeant was different, but when this complaint was made to this young man possessing an old man's mind, it clumsily became known to the public. This problem was brought to the townsman Shinsaburo because the possibility of harakiri was absurd.

"I've told you the reason. Heiji, will you give this your all?"

Sasano Shinsaburo looked hard with renewed hope at young Heiji's face.

"That is awful, but if it is the work of Kazetaro, it should be returned in three days."

"That's impossible."

"Why?"

"Today is the fifth day since the theft. Kazetaro's eyes seemed to have been on the fortune of two thousand ryo."

"It's not that."

"You have taken up the cause of Kazetaro, but do you expect him to return?"

"Would it be possible for me to enter and inspect Akai-sama's mansion?"

"That's no problem. Later on, I will advise that a detective called Heiji will pay a visit."

"Well then, I will go."

"Ah, Heiji, the date of departure of Lord Akai is only three days away. If the two chests aren't returned by then, sadly, Lord Akai will be obliged to commit harakiri. Do you understand?"

"Say no more. This is a matter of life and death and my last chance. I will arrest Kazetaro."

Zenigata Heiji worked up a sweat in his run from Hatchobori to Kobinata on the early summer day.

6

THE VASSAL AKAI SAMON was an exemplary man having an unlucky year at forty-two. He had sufficient pedigree and a fine appearance, but the intensity of his slight quick temper was a flaw. When young, his temper led to many problems, but, as expected, he gained control of his temper after passing forty. Recently, he served close to the shogun Iemitsu and was considered valuable.

"Heiji, you may face unexpected trouble, but I'll leave it to your discretion."

"Yessir."

A lord with twenty-eight hundred koku had no reason to learn about the tricks of a thief. Heiji appeared before Samon once but listened to the steward Ashio Kinai describe the situation that day from many perspectives.

The stolen gold koban coins worth two thousand ryo had been placed in a sealed chest with metal on all sides. Together with the letter signed by the shogun, they decorated the alcove of the inner room. Ashio Kinai, the young samurai of the clan, and their followers took turns keeping watch from the adjacent room.

One chest weighed forty pounds from the gold coins inside. Adding the chest increased the weight to forty-five pounds. Together, the two chests weighed ninety pounds. Strength was needed to carry them.

According to Ashio Kinai, chains remained on the gates and the wooden doors. Therefore, unless escorted while on the estate, he didn't believe a villain could scale the fence and escape. The only people living on the grounds were the vassals and followers of Akai Samon's clan. Only honest people, including the sandal bearers and other workers, were called from the Chiba domain. None of them should have harbored sinister notions.

It would have been a near-miraculous feat for the villain to hug two chests weighing ninety pounds, climb over a nine-foot fence, and escape. If Kazetaro were the pretty, young woman rumored in the world, then how would that happen?

Heiji folded his arms and thought.

"Garappachi, climb over that fence."

"Okay."

"Aren't you confident in your lightness in weight and in spirit? You should be able to do it."

"It's not that I can't do it. I don't feel right acting like a thief."

"Don't worry. Pretend and be praised."

Garappachi gave in and leaped onto the fence. The fence was high, but he was able to crawl up from the inside.

"Okay. I thought climbing over the fence was good, but it's a bad idea."

"Captain, stop joking."

"Wait a minute, this time hold these two rocks and climb over. You can either hold them or carry them on your back."

"That's impossible, Captain."

"Try anyway. If you safely climb over, the rocks will be on this side. Carrying something the weight of a pickled radish is good."

"Stop teasing."

While Heiji kept joking, Garappachi was well aware of the seriousness of his task and tried to scale the wall carrying the two rocks on his back. He tried various schemes, but could not scale the fence with the forty-pound load on his back. Heiji caught Garappachi when he looked in danger of falling backward.

"All right, that's enough. You did your best. Come over here."

As they left, Heiji gave a slight bow to Akai Samon watching from the veranda.

"Lord, the chests could not have been carried off the estate," said Heiji.

"What?"

Samon's eyes opened wide.

"It's strange that nothing has been returned after three days. Because Kazetaro is probably not a demon, even if he somehow scaled that fence, he would have to set one down, or set it on top of the fence, or throw it over to the other side. On the side where Kazetaro may have climbed, there was not the slightest trace of that. If a heavy chest had been placed on the soft field over there, there would be a clear impression."

"Hmm."

"Kazetaro works frighteningly fast, but some say the thief may be a woman. She would surely lack great strength. For that reason, as I said, the two chests were not carried off the grounds."

"Of course, that may be so. I'll leave it to the expert. However, where could he have hidden the chests? Do you intend to search inside the mansion?" asked an enthusiastic Akai Samon.

"Did you inspect that fountain?" asked Heiji.

"Hmm, I don't know."

When Heiji heard that, he did not delay another moment. When the attendants and young samurai pulled up the floodgate, water flooded in and churned around. Although covered in mud, the two chests had been sunk inside and were now in plain sight.

7

HOWEVER, THE JOY DID NOT last for long. The chests were cleaned, and the seals fixed. Finally, it was the eve of the departure. Akai Samon's residence was attacked one more time by the Phantom Thief.

The article stolen this time and what should have been given to Saint Kuya was the letter signed by the shogun Iemitsu. Akai Samon withered because, unlike the chests of coins, this was irreplaceable.

Shinsaburo said, "It was not easy to attack the Akai residence a second time. I regret this, Heiji."

"I do too," said Heiji.

"The signed letter was not easily obtained. You've worked very hard, but please try again."

"Yessir."

Without being told, Heiji rushed out like an eager foal. He imagined this would be his final contest against the Phantom Thief Kazetaro without interference from others and ran unaware of the trembling of his whole body with excitement.

He left Sasano Shinsaburo and went out to the streets of Hatchobori. He flipped his usual brass coin for divination. He caught the falling coin in his palm. When he opened his hand, Heiji said, "Good luck is coming. Great!"

When he brought both sleeves together with a pop to slap his shoulders, his pace to Kobinata quickened.

He arrived at the Akai mansion and guided by Ashio Kinai searched every corner of the residence. This situation was completely different from the chests. It couldn't be sunk in the fountain to keep it from being seen.

Heiji met with the master Samon and asked, "Do you recall anyone with a grudge?"

When young, Samon was famous for his quick temper and willfulness. Where had the grudge originated? He had no idea. Akai Samon was discouraged and seemed troubled when he answered.

"Hachi, go outside," said Heiji.

"What? Is there gonna be a fight?" asked Garappachi.

"Dummy. Don't say stupid things. You probably heard about my blunder with the manju at the tea master's home the other day. Go outside and watch. There is nothing for you to do in the house."

"Hey, Captain, that's something only you'd think of."

"Stop joking."

The two split up. One went to the front and the other to the back to watch the two entrances. Heiji borrowed the storefront of the dealer in household goods to watch the back gate. Garappachi lay down in a grassy field to watch the front gate.

Some hours later, Heiji was given shade and bitter tea through the kindness of the wife of the household goods dealer. Like a clumsy stray dog, Garappachi hiding in the field in Kobinata became so dehydrated with the sun beating down on him he was close to fainting.

About the time the sun began to go down, the young rascals from the neighborhood ran up to the back gate of Akai Samon.

Heiji suddenly saw a scrap of paper held in a hand.

"Ah!"

He flew out of the shop. Taking no notice of the children, he quickly scanned both sides of the street.

He headed to the right in the direction of Myogadani. A lone woman was watching the mischievous children.

"There! he thought and took off running.

The woman saw him and disappeared as if sucked from the street corner.

"Did she escape?"

In the short time Heiji covered thirty steps to reach the corner, the fleeing woman was gone. In her place, a local girl stood on the other side of the street and rushed across the street toward Heiji.

"Oh!"

Nearly colliding, the two jumped back.

"Excuse me, I have a question. Did you see a young woman run away from here just now?"

"No."

The girl seemed to smile and passed close to Heiji to cross the narrow road to the other side.

"Wait," said Heiji and grabbed hold of her obi sash from behind.

"What are you—?"

"Calm down. You are the villain called Kazetaro."

"Huh?"

"Your performance of pretending to escape and doubling back would not be possible by an ordinary person. And your voice is familiar."

Heiji heard this woman's voice once before when he was at the counter at Kasusaya in Harukicho.

"No, you're mistaken."

"Come quietly."

The silvery truncheon with a red tassel glimmered in Heiji's hand.

"Garappachi come here. She's under arrest."

"Ah, thank goodness. When hit by the evening dew, the persimmon *mochi* cake of humanity succeeds."

Garappachi dashed out of the grassy field in front and ran up like a faithful puppy.

He said, "Hey, this is an important matter. That Kazetaro is this young girl?"

Heiji said, "I believe so."

"How sad she ended up a thief."

"You idiot, what are you saying?"

However, Heiji found no reason to disagree with Garappachi's words. The beauty of the young woman with her hands tied behind her back and standing in the sun was breathtaking. She looked captivating with her hair loosely tied up, her patterned satin damask obi, and her tidy, cotton-lined kimono in a style worn about town. She seemed to overflow with purity and beauty.

8

THE SHOGUN'S LETTER WAS returned, and the villain was captured. Akai Samon's mansion filled with cheer like a flower blooming in the evening sun.

The shogun's letter given to the children by the woman was soon returned to Akai Samon. He purified his hands to look at the letter. He saw similarities to the shogun's letter, but the paper was a daring fake.

"Oh! Call Heiji."

Heiji had taken the young woman thief to an inner room for cross-examination and was called back right away by Akai Samon.

"Heiji, this letter is a fake."

"What?"

"Tomorrow's departure is approaching. If it's delayed and this becomes public, this crime of negligence will not be overlooked. Cutting my stomach is easy work, but the shogun's letter has been sullied, and the clan name of Akai will cease. I could not bear that. Heiji, I am asking you again for your help."

The lord with twenty-eight hundred koku could only put his hands together to implore the detective.

"…"

Heiji brooded in silence.

"If the letter is not returned by tomorrow morning, I will be alive only to meet with you. Even if the woman has to be tortured, question her and find that letter."

This seems somewhat violent, but another consideration was this case could not become public and taken to the town magistrate's office.

"Lord, if you please, I would like to borrow your garden to question the woman. Please be present as a witness."

Heiji withdrew pulling the woman to the garden. Under the order of Akai Samon, paper lanterns were hung from poles in the garden, tubs were stacked, and woven straw mats were spread out to create a court of law. The garden gate was opened wide to the street.

While Heiji loathed bringing the matter to court, what else could be done? The announcement made in town was a woman thief entered the mansion to steal and hide an important object, and she will be made to confess and reveal its location. The bored people of the leisure class peculiar to Yamanote flooded in through the gate saying, "This looks interesting." Because a vassal with twenty-eight hundred koku and the famous detective Zenigata Heiji were participants, these people would not be displeased with an unlawful whipping.

The half-naked woman was forced to sit on the straw mat laid out in the middle of the garden and tied to a green bamboo stake pushed through the mat.

Akai Samon stood at the entrance where shoes are removed, Zenigata Heiji, Garappachi, and the attendants stood at the front of the entrance to begin this cruel spectacle.

"Woman, you are without a doubt the thief known as Kazetaro who has disrupted society lately. Where did you hide the article stolen from this mansion? In any case, you will be handed over to the town police sergeant for your punishment. However, before that, you must return the article taken from the mansion. If you confess without hesitation..."

The steward Ashio Kinai bent forward slightly and with all his might struck the back of the bamboo the woman was lashed to with a bamboo sword.

The woman was gagged to muffle her screams or shrieks. With each strike by the sword, the white flesh of the top half of her half-naked body trembled. Her breasts twisted and bent from her shoulders cut into by the straw rope.

"You're too kind Kinai. Hit her harder," said Akai Samon.

Heiji said, "Let me do it. Well, woman?"

Heiji took and raised high the bamboo sword. This detective was an extraordinary human man and had been dubbed Bungling Heiji, but would willingly whip the tender flesh of the bound young woman.

Beneath the dim light of the hanging lights, fifty to sixty townsmen, who pushed in, averted their eyes from the harsh scene, and whispers of condemnation came in waves.

"If you wish to speak, nod your head three times, then I'll remove the gag. Where did you hide the important article?"

Heiji's bamboo sword continued to echo on the woman's back. Her body writhed in agony, nonetheless, she did not reveal the location.

"Lord, please kill this woman cut by cut. If not, she will seal her mouth."

"Very well," said Akai Samon and slipped on his garden geta sandals and stepped down. To his right was a new blade and reflected the flame to shine brilliantly like a branding iron.

9

"W.AIT!"

A man dashed out from the spectators and pushed aside Garappachi and the attendants to stand with arms wide in front of the woman.

"Who are you?" demanded Akai Samon.

"I am known to the world as the Phantom Thief Kazetaro," he said without hesitation and stared hard at Akai Samon and Zenigata Heiji. He was forty-five or -six years old with a small, slender build, but had some mystery within his air of cunning of a cross between a merchant and a gambler.

"Arrest the scoundrel!"

The man looked with contempt at Garappachi as he leaped forward.

"Calm down. I will introduce myself and not attempt to hide or escape."

He calmly placed his hands in his kimono.

Heiji said, "Your name was Kazetaro. Sangoro, if you have a reason, we're listening."

"As expected, Heiji speaks with wisdom. In a clumsy struggle, the shogun's letter in my kimono would be mutilated," said Sangoro.

The villain's and the detective's eyes met and gauged each other's breaths. Akai Samon, Ashio Kinai, and Garappachi were invisible to them. Sangoro was a sporting man who made a little name for himself in Kuramae. The identity of the Phantom Thief Kazetaro surprised Heiji.

"All right, Heiji, you'll probably understand. Listen. Here's the reason."

"..."

While shielding the young woman, Sangoro's Kazetaro lowered his voice and said,

"What is the cause and effect? I have a sickness that makes me steal. My body is lightweight and my intelligence is average, but my enemy is I must steal any object I see that looks beyond human ability to steal. I was born with this weakness.

"I was fine while my wife was alive. However, after she died three years ago, I was unable to suppress my kleptomania. As you know, my life is not hard, and I didn't steal for want of money. I had no interest in the money or any of the items I stole. This young woman worried about my habit and offered many suggestions, but nothing worked. She eventually gave up but returned what I stole to the original owner. I worried when I heard the rumor that Kazetaro was a woman thief. You understand, Heiji."

Heiji and Samon did not speak after hearing this mysterious story. Sangoro was unfazed and continued looking at their appalled faces.

"However, the only objects I didn't return were the chests of one thousand ryo and the shogun's letter stolen from this mansion. My reason would take a long time to explain. In short, when Akai Samon was young, he used sake to shield his gaffes. In the middle of cherry blossom viewing in Sumidazutsumi, he rudely began to attack me. Fortunately, my life was saved at a dangerous moment. Here is the scar he gave me on that occasion."

He stuck out his face to show a scar from a sword that gave him the nickname of Side Scar Sangoro. A slanted red line was drawn from the forehead to the cheek of the fortyish man.

"Now, you can understand my plan to make Akai Samon cut himself open. The chests were too heavy, so I sunk them in the fountain, but you found them. So I stole the shogun's letter. The young lady still had mercy. Because it was obvious she would return the object to its owner, I deliberately made a fake and she was arrested. That became my undoing. The suffering of the woman by your actions was the failure of my life. Do you understand, Heiji? What was the reason a popular fellow called Bungling Heiji rained down such brutality on this young woman? Until now, I was aggravated that I had too high an opinion of you. You must feel anger toward me, too, Heiji."

"Sangoro, look at the woman. If there is a scar, even one resembling a poke from a cormorant's feather, I will place both hands on the ground in apology," said Heiji.

"What?"

"This ploy lured in you and everyone else. When you heard she was arrested, you were sure to come to this place."

"Dammit."

"Now, the story is over. I will put down the letter and go home with the young lady. Lord Akai will confess his youthful mistake," said Sangoro. When he turned around, Akai Samon looked ashamed and bowed in silence toward him.

"In fact, you should be tied up and hauled away, but if you go away and stay out of my sight, you will be excused. Do you understand, Sangoro?" asked Heiji.

"Yes."

Sangoro fell silent for a short time and compared the wholesome face of the young woman tied to the bamboo stake and the faces bearing no hostility belonging to Samon and Heiji.

ZENIGATA HEIJI ADDED ANOTHER failure. The Phantom Thief Sangoro, aka Kazetaro, left for parts unknown. On the following day, Akai Samon set off on his journey to the capital.

"Heiji, the thief appears to have escaped again. That interfered with your favorite pastime, too," chided Sasano Shinsaburo sounding sweetly nostalgic.

"Yessir."

Heiji prostrated himself and said nothing.

CHAPTER FOUR

CURSE OF THE ORNAMENTAL HAIRPINS

1

I'VE BEEN IN THIS TRADE for a long time, but seeing a murder victim will always be dreadful," said Zenigata Heiji, like he was repeating a favorite saying. Handling a bloodstained body is the fate of being in his business, but Heiji's nerves were too sensitive.

He found this unbearable because he had to look at the most gruesome corpse without being able to flee.

"Garappachi, you've brought me to a horrible place. I'll have to endure."

"The mistake in roping off the crime scene was on purpose. The proprietor of Hoteiya had doubts about Captain Ishihara and asked for Zenigata to take a look."

"Meddling is tiresome."

Heiji smacked his lips, but didn't turn to go home. He parted the rattan screen of the houseboat moored on the Yanagibashi side. Inside was a sea of blood.

When Heiji looked under the obscure light of the lantern held out by his sidekick Garappachi, a young geisha had a silver ornamental hairpin plunged deep into her right eye and had died lying down.

"Eeyah!"

Heiji hated dead bodies and reflexively averted his eyes. She was young and pretty. Half her face was smeared with blood, but it wasn't hideous.

"This was cruel."

Heiji returned to being conscious of his work and moved one step closer to the corpse.

When he straightened her bare leg that had kicked back her crimson skirt, her hand caught his eye.

"What's that in her hand?"

Garappachi had not noticed. Heiji quickly approached and saw the cord of a man's half-length *haori* coat clutched in her left hand twisted by agony. It was made of a thick, short braided silk popular at the time. The cord seemed to have been loosened and wrenched out during a quarrel and torn off with a loop.

"This is a good clue."

With a little pride, Garappachi picked up the discarded haori coat with its silk cord torn off.

The woman's bangs were messy like they had been grabbed from behind and yanked, but there were no visible wounds.

The ornamental hairpin stuck in her eye was a sturdy, flattened metal with a shallow carving of a hawk's wing but too unrefined an object for adorning a geisha's hair.

Heiji suddenly realized that the object was about four inches long like a pine needle. Therefore, to be pushed into an eye without using a hammer, phenomenal strength was required. He wondered how she was stabbed.

"Captain, the master of Hoteiya wishes to speak to you," said a professional jester Kinbei as he gave a slight bow from the shore and cautiously looked into the boat. He was a member of the party out enjoying the cool evening air.

"Did he ask to see me?"

"Yes."

Heiji nodded and gazed at the face of the woman so cruelly killed. Mysteriously, a tortoiseshell comb and an ornamental hairpin fitted with five coral jewels in fine metal did not shatter and remained intact.

2

A LUMBER WHOLESALER IN KOMAGATA, Hoteiya Manzaburo, who would appear on either page two or three of a list of the wealthiest men in Edo, brought along a familiar young geisha and a town dance master Sai on a boat outing from Komagata to enjoy the cool evening air.

The boarding party totaled six, including the professional jesters. The boatman Naosuke leisurely rowed and landed at Yanagibashi a little before ten. Among the items carried onto the boat, quite a bit of the sake had not been consumed. Their stomachs were empty, and they would drink again at

Tsuruyoshi on the riverbank. The party crossed over the jetty and entered the cottage through the back gate of Tsuruyoshi.

The geisha was young and pretty and most sought after in Yoshiwara. When forced to drink, she became tipsy. She was unaccustomed to drinking, started babbling, and in the end, was left on the boat. After they gulped down the sake, the drunken geisha and the boatman Naosuke with unsteady hands for pushing the oars were separated. She was at the bow, and he was at the stern of the moored boat. A cool breeze passing over the water buffeted them.

After an hour passed, Naosuke woke up as if he were under attack. When no guests were around, he quickly got drunk and fell asleep holding the oar.

He thought it was a shame to be separated by a rattan screen from a popular geisha said to be the next Goddess of Mercy. Lately, the pretty geisha was like one of Manzaburo's belongings. The only embarrassment was she was a little young for him.

Naosuke wiped off his drool and straightened his kimono. He peered vacantly toward the bow. The lanterns hanging from both eaves exhausted their candles unnoticed, but that didn't prevent him from looking beyond the rattan screen.

A sea of blood. A silver ornamental hairpin stood erect in her eyeball. Crimson red stained her skirt in disarray.

A brief glance stunned Naosuke.

"Eeyah! Th...this is horrible!"

His drowsiness and drunkenness vanished. He raced to the Tsuruyoshi cottage.

He was shaken, confused, and wasn't sure what to do. Some time passed before someone ran to the offices of the town officials.

Fortunately, Heiji, the famous criminal catcher, and his sidekick Garappachi, on his way home from a gathering, were known to be enjoying drinks in front of Tsuruyoshi and were immediately pulled away. They were repeatedly refused entry to the scene, but an error in roping off the scene allowed them to look over the scene before the arrival of the town officials to investigate the death.

"Captain, this is it. Please have a look around."

As a property owner, he believed a private detective or a police detective had to be coaxed. Manzaburo, the master of Hoteiya, gently slipped five or six gold coins twisted inside tissue paper into Heiji's sleeve.

"Oh no! What are you doing? That's not necessary, rather, it is wrong," said Heiji in a quiet, modest tone and returned the package of coins to Manzaburo's hand. Today (Showa year 6 [1931]), the market price of those five or six coins would rival two or three hundred yen and be more than enough to purchase a greedy police detective. However, Manzaburo had difficulty gauging Heiji's mood and wondered whether a little more was needed.

Heiji paid no attention to the details and looked over the group of uneasy faces lined up on the balcony. Hoteiya Manzaburo was thirty-seven or -eight years old with a blank expression. He was also a fine, kindhearted man who had the look, although slightly garish, of a wealthy merchant of the time. However, he did not have the constitution to wield a silver ornamental hairpin to kill a woman.

With him were two professional jesters and the young woman with the job of warming the sake. They may have been there to swipe food to eat on the sly and slip away into the night, but not to kill a human being.

From the shadow of Manzaburo's sleeve, a pale face cramped by terror was the dance master Sai, a twenty-seven or eight-year-old woman approaching middle age. She was a beautiful woman who carried herself like a businesswoman. However, she was not the type to drive a four-inch hairpin into someone's eye.

Finally, there was the boatman Naosuke, who was still onboard the boat. He was around thirty years old, single, and a nice man but a bad drunk. In the search for suspects, he would be in first place.

With arms folded, Heiji deliberated.

The evening breeze crossing the river was chilly for June. The quietness of Edo a little past the first watch managed to penetrate the body.

At that moment, a man said, "Zenigata-san, thank you for your hard work. Now that we're here, you may go."

He spoke sharply and stared coldly. When Heiji raised his head, the brazen face of the fortyish man that appeared from behind the group belonged to Ishihara Risuke, Heiji's rival in great exploits.

3

"Heiji."

"Yes."

"I'm sorry for making you come here."

"It's fine. What is the problem?"

Heiji was called to the mansion of young Sergeant Sasano Shinsabura and looked up from outside the door threshold. The gap in status between the police sergeant and the officer kept Heiji from even considering entering the mansion without permission.

"Come in Heiji. I wish to ask you something."

"Yessir."

"Obviously, I want to ask about the killing of the Yanagibashi geisha. Ishihara Risuke came to a conclusion and arrested Hoteiya Manzaburo, but he doesn't seem to be the culprit."

"What? That arrest is illegal. No, it's wrong to say Ishihara-san's judgment was in error, but Manzaburo had no reason to kill her."

Heiji left much unsaid, but he sounded excited.

"Oh, what do you mean? Without an understanding of the proper facts, you would have no reason to say that sort of thing. Tell me your thoughts."

"Yessir," said a bewildered Heiji. He did not have one piece of undisputed evidence, but his sixth sense was pinging.

"Manzaburo dropped coins in your sleeve that night. Didn't that anger you?"

Where had he heard that? Shinsaburo saw through to the slightest matters.

"Yessir."

"Being unaware of your character was Manzaburo's error. Acting so despicably, I believe there may be guilty feelings in Manzaburo."

"Sir, your thinking may be in error."

"In what way?"

"If the murderer were the very wealthy Manzaburo, he would not shut a detective's mouth with three or five ryo. He would be resolved to hand out a surprisingly huge amount of money like fifty or one-hundred ryo."

"Of course."

"Manzaburo pushed the package of three or five ryo at me but ended up mystified. Hearing the detective was an affable man, he was not acting as an audacious villain, but as a cowardly businessman."

"Hmmm, Risuke made a terrible mistake, but it was not unimaginable."

Sasano Shinsaburo had a sudden realization but was not betrayed by his words.

Heiji said, "If reasons arise to suspect Manzaburo, as a precaution, please tell me. But I do have an opinion, may I tell you a little of what I saw?"

"Well, I wondered why the cord ripped off from Manzaburo's haori coat was in the hand of the murdered woman? According to Risuke, that was the best proof..." said Sasano Shinsaburo implying that could not be explained away.

Heiji said, "That is strange, but the woman's bangs were a mess and looked like they had been pulled. The hair became that way because the villain grabbed her hair from behind and plunged the hairpin carried in his right hand into her right eye. Was the frantic woman able to wrench out the cord from the haori coat of the villain behind her?"

"Hmmmm," said Shinsaburo who was convinced by Heiji without resorting to showy gestures.

"Also, it was strange to leave the haori coat with the ripped cord behind."

"..."

"One more thing, according to the servants at Tsuruyoshi I later questioned, they said when the party first left the boat and entered the cottage, Manzaburo was not wearing a haori coat. Given that, Manzaburo slipped out of the cottage, returned to the boat, put his coat on, and then killed the woman. After that, he took off the haori coat with the ripped cord and left it on the boat."

"I see. Heiji, I too find that hard to believe. Risuke said he was certain about Manzaburo, but when the maid at Tsuruyoshi was questioned, she said Manzaburo got up once to relieve himself. The maid was with him at that time and said he did not leave the gathering early."

"I heard that, too."

"Risuke said Manzaburo's wealth enabled him to shut the mouths of a few maids."

"That is an outrage. The living proof may be three to five people. Until their stories are identical, everyone is a suspect."

The two men exchanged looks and got lost in their own thoughts. If Manzaburo were not the murderer, who committed that cruel act?

"Heiji, thanks to you, I understand much more. Risuke said, tomorrow, even if torture is used, Manzaburo will confess. Under these circumstances, there is no reason for that to proceed. I ask you not to hold back and do your best to work with Risuke."

"Yessir," said the perplexed Heiji and dropped his eyes to his knees.

4

THE FOLLOWING DAY MANZABURO was pardoned.

"Captain, Ishihara Risuke arrested the boatman Naosuke," said the scatterbrained Garappachi in a voice that echoed throughout the row house as he came running.

"He finally did it? I thought he would."

Heiji flung his tobacco pipe on the tatami and tightened his folded arms.

"Hey Captain, do you think the boatman is the killer?"

"I don't know."

"Is the charge false?"

"I don't know that either. No matter how drunk he may have been, it's strange he didn't realize someone had been killed on the other side of a rattan screen."

"Thinking about it, just as Ishihara expected, the murderer was the boatman without a doubt."

"If the boatman wanted to kill the geisha, without waving around the troublesome ornamental hairpin, he simply would snatch her legs and sink her in the river."

"Of course."

"If not, a blade should be on the boat."

"..."

"Wouldn't a hatchet or a kitchen knife be more useful than a hairpin?"

"If that's so..."

"If the boatman actually killed her, why wasn't he more devious? Getting drunk, falling asleep, and knowing nothing is not a clever plan."

"You may be right," said the dim Garappachi who did not have a single clue.

The duo returned to Yanagibashi. They intentionally landed the boat downstream of Tsuruyoshi. As the party did the other night, they opened the wicker gate and passed into the cottage. Inside the boat, nothing was gained other than discovering the ability to go back and forth along a stonewall at the shore.

They walked around to haberdashers in the neighborhood to show them the ornamental hairpin pulled from the geisha's eye.

"I'm sorry, but I don't recall selling this recently? This hairpin is an old style. It looks like an article passed down two or three generations. Finding a haberdasher in Edo with this item would be difficult. If you look at the wear of that seal or trace of a hawk's feather, this article was probably made thirty to fifty years ago?"

All the haberdashers said nearly the same thing. This discouraged further investigations by the pair.

When they returned disappointed, Heiji's elderly hired maid was anxiously standing outside and said to Heiji, "Captain, you have a guest."

"Who?"

"A woman."

"A woman? Now, that's strange."

"Captain, you two must be more than friends."

"Garappachi, that's a dumb thing to say."

5

HIS GUEST WAS AN ATTRACTIVE, twenty-four- or -five-year-old woman approaching middle age with blue traces for eyebrows. She was stuffed into an unlined checkered kimono with a satin obi sash like a small mountain and resembled a sloppy housekeeper. She was shedding bitter tears.

"Are you Captain Zenigata? Please excuse my rudeness by coming inside to wait."

When she spoke in an eloquent tone and smiled, he glimpsed her jet-black teeth. Her lips looked like they could hurl curses, but she seemed uncommonly coquettish.

"I'm sorry I was not here to greet you. May I ask, who are you?"

Although it was his home, Heiji felt welcoming her was awkward as he went inside to bring her a tobacco tray and a seat cushion.

"There is nothing else. It's about that Yoshihara geisha killed in Yanagibashi. I would like to ask the captain about her."

"..."

"The murderer has already been arrested? I may be a bit pushy, but I have a reason for coming here to ask you these questions."

She seemed to have difficulty speaking, but managed to speak eloquently and looked up alluringly at Heiji's face looking down at her.

"No, not at all, this is a problem because I don't have a clue. You should go to Ishihara Risuke and ask him. He may have found something."

"Oh, I haven't asked Captain Ishihara."

She smiled as if concealing something and stood.

"Are you leaving now?"

"I will visit another time. I am sorry for the intrusion."

"Oh, wait. What is your name? And your address?"

"No, that's not necessary. If I have business, I will come again. Goodbye Captain."

She gave a slight polite bow and slipped out the door to the alley.

"Hachi."

"Yes?"

"After her."

"Okay."

Garappachi flew out to follow the woman. He returned a short time later looking bewitched.

"What happened, Hachi?"

"Captain, she's not human. When I ran out to the alley, did she go right or left? I couldn't tell."

"What do you mean?"

"She vanished like smoke."

"Did you see any vehicles?"

"Maybe I was careless, but there was only one vehicle I could name. A fine palanquin passed from the right to the left."

"That was it."

"Oh?"

"The woman got into a palanquin waiting a distance away on the right and passed to the left. What a dope. You never noticed."

"Oh yeah!" Garappachi said but didn't understand.

When Heiji looked at the traces left behind by the woman, she appeared to have rummaged around in his absence. He kept a notebook in a drawer of his chest. He was disturbed because he wrote down every detail from the case of the murdered geisha to his expectations in that notebook. When he called to the maid who let the woman in his house, she was flustered and offered no help.

6

ALTHOUGH HEIJI'S INTUITION KNEW the boatman was not the murderer, he had no evidence to counter and push back at Ishihara Risuke.

The next day, the tearful mother of the boatman Naosuke rushed to Heiji's home. "Please save my son. He's a bit of a bad drinker, but in his heart, he's an honest man like a god. He's not a man who kills."

Because these words came from his mother, she might have been exaggerating or conceited. However, Heiji may have agreed about the boatman's innocence.

Nevertheless, he went forward with evidence that failed to advance the case. After stopping Ishihara Risuke, Heiji had to think of a way to save Naosuke's life.

Still crying, his mother returned home. Had she visited Heiji to seek comfort, but instead, lost hope?

Her sorrow could not continue forever. She half-heartedly claimed the murderer of the geisha was not the boatman Naosuke but offered no proof of her claim.

No traces remain today, but in front of the gate of Houroku Jizo-sama in Kawara-machi, which was popular in those days was the *Ohyakudo-ishi* prayer rock. Beside it, Koma, the daughter of a yarn seller in the same town, had a silver ornamental hairpin pushed into her right eyeball, just like the geisha, and suffered the same cruel death.

Koma was a town girl, who just turned seventeen, said in song and in pictures to have beauty without equal from Asakusa to Ryogoku. Her deep devotion might have led her to visit the shrine at night. All of Edo was in an uproar because her pitiful corpse with a punctured eyeball was discovered beneath the prayer rock of Houroku Jizo-sama.

Risuke and Heiji, and even the town police sergeant Sasano Shinsabura raced to the scene. The method was identical to the killing of the geisha in Yanagibashi. Not even a clue like a strand of hair remained.

Koma wore an unlined kimono with a gaudy embroidered design. Her obi sash charmingly tied in back had been pulled, and half of her body was dyed a deep red. The pain of her death brought tears to eyes accustomed to death.

"Risuke, Heiji, this is serious and not a time to fight for achievements. Combine your hearts and find this killer. Soon the public unrest will reach the ears of the shogun," said a stern Shinsaburo.

The embarrassed Heiji and Risuke said nothing.

The boatman Naosuke was released within the day. Risuke no longer had a target to tie up.

Later, third and fourth victims appeared. The third victim was San, a pretty girl who enticed customers to the drinking establishment of Okuramae. On her way home from a public bath, she was stabbed in the eye with a silver ornamental hairpin at the entrance to the garden of a teahouse. The fourth victim was Kuni, the young wife of a haberdasher in Komagata. While waiting for her husband who was out on business, she closed the shop early and went inside. There, she was stabbed in the right eye with a hairpin. Her tragic corpse lay beside an oblong brazier.

The technique did not vary in the least for the four victims. However, when looking at how the murderer approached each victim, the murderer must have lived in the neighborhood and been known to the victims. Another characteristic was the murdered women were seventeen to twenty-five years old and differed only slightly in age and social status. All were known beauties, not one could be deemed average.

In those days, they said young women were afraid to go out alone at night and truly beautiful women were terrified. Throughout Edo, the turmoil seethed and boiled over.

After being summoned by Magistrate Asakura Iwanami-no-kami of Minami-cho, Sergeant Sasano Shinsaburo put pressure on Risuke and Heiji and made these cases a priority, but no news emerged from their competition for great achievements.

7

"CAPTAIN, OF THESE FOUR ORNAMENTAL hairpins, only two were flattened metal of genuine silver, but the other two were unexpected fakes, silver plating on a brass base."

"What?"

This surprised Zenigata Heiji, too. The four hairpins used to kill the four women were borrowed from a government office. That was the expert opinion of a metalsmith acquaintance.

However, the surprise of silver-plating was a ray of hope shining in Heiji's heart.

Heiji had Garappachi return the important evidence of hairpins to the government office. He went to the bustling downtown of Ryogoku.

Needless to say, the crowds in Ryogoku at that time resemble Ward 6 in Asakusa today in Showa year 6. Freak shows, acrobats, and kabuki theaters stood side by side. Roadside teahouses were built between them and lured in the passers-by. Street vendors wedged into the few empty lots. There were top spinners, men drawing swords and cutting down rivals, and hack magic tricks to draw in a crowd for the fast talkers straining their voices to hawk cheap toys and potatoes turned to stone by Kobo-sama.

Mixed in among them was an outdoor stall for silver-plating. A mat was spread on the street. A multitude of hardware having various sizes — metal basins, bells, metal charcoal-handling tongs, kettles, coins, keys — was arranged on top. Supposedly, they were polished with weak tea powder to a brilliant silver color.

"Please look closely. The secret process of this silver-plating was passed from a Dutchman. There's nothing else like it here or there. When a little spit is applied, any object immediately becomes silver. Fragments of pots, copper kettles, brass tobacco pipes, anything, they're all the same. If you wish, right before your eyes, a bright gold coin will become splendid sparkling silver. Those who think I'm a liar, give me a pipe, or an ornamental hairpin, or whatever you're carrying and behold. Don't be shy."

He was surprised to see the woman speaking so glibly was the woman who visited Heiji's home while he was out the other day. She asked awkwardly for clues about the scoundrel who used hairpins to kill and had stolen his notebook. He was not confused by the astounding beauty of the mature woman.

However, Heiji did not reveal his metal truncheon in the crowd and ignite mayhem in the busy area at noontime.

He took out a hand towel to partially cover his head. From the safety of the crowd, he closely watched every action of the mysterious woman and missed nothing.

There was another surprise. When he looked closely at the various metal objects arranged on the mat, he could safely say they were all objects stolen from this neighborhood, plated with silver, and lined up before everyone. This was the height of dishonesty.

Her actions were brazen. Among these objects were bronze incense burners, waxed silver figurines, a masterpiece of a sword guard and sword hilt ornament, and worst of all, even genuine gold coins and silver nuggets were mixed in. Each one, even fragments from pots and kettle lids were silver-plated.

Heiji was thoroughly absorbed, did not leave the area, and watched the beauty of silver-plating for half a day. In the evening, when the pedestrian traffic thinned, the woman quickly closed up shop and carried on her back the stolen goods and trash tossed in a bamboo basket and wrapped in a large wrapping cloth. She rolled up the mat and carried it under her arm and briskly hauled all her wares to Yaganibashi.

8

AROUND TWILIGHT, THE PEDESTRIANS disappeared, and the tradesmen's homes and the water were dyed a uniform reddish brown. When she reached the desolate shore in Yaganibashi, "Excuse me, Madam, please wait a moment."

Heiji could not stop himself from calling to her.

"What? That is unnerving. Do you have business with me?"

"Yes."

"I will not permit any offensive acts. Excuse me, but I am Roku, a silver plater."

She had difficulty gauging what he expected to learn from her. The woman called Roku peered at him through the evening twilight.

"Roku, you're under arrest. Come quietly," said Heiji and flashed his truncheon.

"Ah, it's you. Heiji."

Roku jumped back and managed to free her shoulder. Her heavy load fell to the grass. She quickly turned a willow into a small shield.

"Roku, you can't escape. Surrender and let me tie you up."

"What? The hands of a cheap detective will not touch the silver plater Roku. If you put up a poor fight, you'll be stabbed by thorns."

"Shut up!"

Heiji jumped and whacked her shoulder.

"Ow!"

He grabbed her wrist as she tried to escape and soon had his policeman's rope around it.

"I applaud you."

This result was not because Roku was weak, but because Heiji's skill was brilliant. Before three night laborers could stop walking, the beautiful silver plater had been expertly tied up by Zenigata Heiji.

He took the bound woman and her bundle to the local guardhouse. He slammed shut the shoji door and waved away the dust.

"Woman, there's nothing you can do but confess everything to me."

"Heiji, don't get full of yourself. Investigations are the work of government officials. A police detective is impertinent to try to talk to Roku," she said breathing hard through her nose in an alluring voice. The mature beauty struggling against the knot was unusual. This could not be handled by ordinary means. Heiji changed to a quick assault.

"Shut up! You killed four young women. You still have some life in you. If you are obedient, the authorities may show mercy."

"What are you saying? Tell me again. I killed four young women? Please stop talking nonsense. I know nothing about any murders. The silver plater Roku has the nature of Buddha and hates to kill an insect. Don't speak such rubbish."

Roku looked surprised.

"Hiding anything will be bad for you. The proof is the silver-plated ornamental hairpins. You first killed the geisha in Yanagibashi and continued to kill with your hands until four women were dead. You are a devil woman."

"What are you saying? In that case, you should speak quickly. Captain Zenigata Heiji is out of his mind."

"What?"

"The geisha killed in Yanagibashi was the younger sister of a blood relative of mine. I have a warped yakuza husband who fell in with night burglars. He was coldhearted and considered her a nuisance to relatives, and, sadly, he killed her."

"…"

"I only thought I wanted to strike at my foe, so I went to your home to find out what you knew because you are famous for capturing criminals. I was wrong to take your notebook, but if I hadn't, you never would have talked to me about clues leading to the murderer."

Heiji's blow was unfortunate. Roku was no different from a bad woman, but he didn't think her recollection with tears rising in her eyes was a lie.

"Very well, I was wrong. I will untie you, not say a word, and look away. I will forgo the triumph of tying up a sneak thief or a cat burglar."

"..."

As Heiji untied the woman's rope, he continued, "Instead, tell me everything. There was probably a woman who recently visited your stall and had you silver plate two brass ornamental hairpins."

"Yes, yes. It was odd. She had me carefully apply silver plating even to ornamental hairpins with metal legs. Because she had no coins, she said to bring the hairpins to the Sujikai Gate by eight tonight when the bell rings to exchange them for money."

"Wh...what?"

9

TWO HOURS LATER...

The silver plater Roku stood in the dim shadows of the wall outside Sujikai Gate.

"Are you the silver plater?"

A woman appeared out of nowhere. Her face could not be seen in the semidarkness, but her cultivated voice reminded him of someone.

"Yes. Miss, I have the hairpins."

"Thank you. Now, we will exchange the hairpins for the payment. There is also a tip."

"Oh, this is too much. Thank you so much."

The woman nimbly moved behind Roku as she gave a slight bow. Her left hand grabbed Roku's bangs from behind.

"Ah!"

She was unusually powerful.

The head of the scoundrel Roku was raised up without resistance and instantly held under her attacker's left arm. A silver hairpin flickering in the dim moonlight shot toward Roku's eye.

"Umph!"

A single coin flew in and smacked into the elbow of the mystery woman as it swung up.

"Eeyah!"

The hairpin hit the gravel with a clang. The mystery woman pushed Roku away and took five or six steps into the darkness.

"Stop! You're under arrest!"

From behind, a truncheon slammed down on the woman's shoulder.

THE MYSTERY WOMAN ARRESTED by Heiji was Sai, the dance master.

This woman had been raised in a samurai family. She had considerable knowledge of martial arts and possessed amazing strength. After reaching marriageable age, she fell into the fast life, became a dance master, and lived incognito.

She later confessed that in the bloom of her youth she was about to be robbed and raped, but escaped the danger by pushing a silver ornamental hairpin into her attacker's eye. Strangely, since that time, she has agonized with the urge to stab people in the eye with a silver hairpin. She wanted to stop, but could not. In today's jargon, she suffered from hysterical paranoia.

At one time, she made a secret vow with Manzaburo, the proprietor of Hoteiya, but resented soon being abandoned for the Yoshihara geisha. On that night, she slipped out of the Tsuruyoshi cottage and returned to the summer pleasure boat. While the dead-drunk captain was dozing, she stabbed the young geisha in the eye and killed her in a daring attack. However, she resorted to the cheap ploy of tearing off the cord from the haori coat of the resented Manzaburo.

If that were the extent of the attacks, perhaps no one would have become suspicious. However, once she yielded to the temptation of the silver ornamental hairpin and saw blood, Sai's deranged mind became eternally mad. If she saw a younger and prettier woman, her mind was besieged by the terrifying temptation and desire to thrust a silver ornamental hairpin into an eye.

The first two victims were killed by genuine silver ornamental hairpins, but none remained for the third and fourth victims. Without the ability to buy more, she comforted her deranged spirit by silver-plating other types of hairpins.

One was used on the fifth victim. A single gold ornamental hairpin, a keepsake from her mother, remained, so she had that hairpin silver-plated to make Roku her final sacrifice.

Zenigata Heiji successfully captured the demon ornamental hairpin killer. Where the silver plater Roku went, no one knows. Police Sergeant Sasano Shinsaburo probably glowered and said, "Heiji, you have failed again."

CHAPTER FIVE

GHOST GIRL

1

"Captain, have you heard?"

"What? Why all the racket?"

Zenigata Heiji's sidekick Garappachi came flying into his house. He clutched his dyed hand towel to wipe sweat from the shaved part of his head to the tip of his nose.

"A terrible thing has happened."

"Is it the story of Princess Hime in pursuit of the handsome priest Anchin again and turning into a serpent at the Hidaka River?"

"This is no joke. Today, I got a better story. The rumor is a funeral has gone out without a corpse for the first time since the founding of Edo."

"What? A funeral without the deceased. Where did that happen?"

Heiji automatically leaned forward. Usually, he took Garappachi's stories with a grain of salt, but the news he brought today may be important enough to spark his curiosity.

"You've heard about the disappearance of Hina, the town belle of Oumiya."

"I heard. On her way home from visiting the Goddess of Mercy, she disappeared before the eyes of the maid accompanying her."

"Did she fall into the ocean and die? Or was she murdered? They say that every evening since the third, she has appeared as a ghost."

"I didn't hear about any ghost story, dummy."

"A dummy has no feelings. It's scary because everyone says it's a true story."

"There should be a reason for having a funeral without a body. Is it just a standard ghost story, or something never seen since the dawn of Edo?"

"But Captain, they say that a ghost is summoned."

"What? Is it summoning a ghost or an extravagant corpse?"

"Without a funeral, the dead will not rest. I want the objects I've prized during my life and the valuable objects among my belongings to be collected, and instead of me, be put in a casket with gold coins worth three hundred ryo, and then all of it buried beside the grave of my ancestors."

"Are you serious?"

"Yes I am, Captain Zenigata doesn't know anything about this town."

"You're an absurd fellow. In the town I live, that sort of person is despised. Garappachi, come with me," said Heiji as he tightened his obi sash, wrapped his shiny truncheon in a towel and placed it at his breast. Then he slipped on his straw sandals and dashed outside.

"Captain, where are we going? I gotta remind you, it's not my fault," said Garappachi surprised by Heiji's enthusiasm.

With a touch of nervousness, Heiji said, "What? No one's saying anything is your fault. Your face does not have the features suited for a ghost. For a haunted mansion in Asakusa, I want to call on an actor with a clean-shaven head."

"Dammit."

"An angry Hachi will guide me straight to Oumiya. A hateful ghost brings grief to parents and swindles large sums of money. Before three days pass, his true character will be revealed to the world."

"That's a scary spirit, Captain."

Zenigata Heiji frowned and said, "Don't forget. I really hate ghosts who use those tricks."

He was young and hot-blooded at the time. From the Kan'ei era to the Meireki and Manji eras, the famous detective, also called Bungling Heiji, was an impressive man.

2

WHEREVER THE ROOF OF KANNON-DO, the temple to the Goddess of Mercy, could be seen, Oumiya Jibei, the proprietor of a pawnbroker and currency exchange shop in Hanakawado, was said to be an exceptional man. He and his wife Toyo had an only daughter Hina. Her amazing looks were believed to have beauty unrivaled by any town maiden in Edo.

Being too beautiful, her parents were overly fastidious and a son-in-law had not been settled on by her eighteenth summer. Dressed in a luxurious large-sleeved kimono, she appeared many times with an attendant on the road and stole many cold hearts in the neighborhood.

One day, she traveled a short distance with her maid Sei to pay a visit to Kannon-sama. When they reached the front of Denpoin Temple, Sei happened to look away for a moment, and Hina vanished.

Was she sucked into the Earth? Had she been transformed into a giant straw *waraji* sandal of the guardian gods of the temple gate? Even if she never considered these possibilities, Sei was astonished by her unbelievable mysterious disappearance. She may have believed Hina played a joke on her when she looked away and returned home alone. Sei returned to the master's house without a care in the world. However, Hina had no reason to return first. Moreover, no one had seen her.

Pandemonium reigned at Oumiya. Headed by the shop manager, clerks and shop boys to merchants with business dealings and the young townspeople were mobilized for a search. Centering on Kannon-sama, they searched every back street and every garbage box in the neighborhood, but no shadow or figure remained where she disappeared.

Was she tempted by some gorgeous demon? Was she kidnapped by a scoundrel to be sold? Did she evaporate like a beautiful rainbow? Rumors gave birth to more rumors with no end.

On the evening of the third day, after the shop's front shutter had been lowered, frantic knocking began. The shop boy Kanekichi went over and opened the window peephole to peek out. In the darkness under the eaves, a woman, who was plainly Hina, stood looking miserable, like she was doused with water. The light from the pale moon hanging over the roof across the street enveloped her in an indescribable dread.

"Oh, Miss!"

As he hurried to open the door, others in the store rushed over. The cold moonlit summer night was bright enough to see a crawling ant. However, Kanekichi no longer saw the figure of Hina there.

"You dope. You saw her in a dream," scolded the clerks. Kanekichi stifled his sobs.

Nevertheless, the head clerks who scolded him saw a square foot of wetness on the dry ground and looked at each other spontaneously.

The following night around two in the morning, the proprietor Jibei recalled the surprising story from the previous evening as he splashed water from the washbasin on his face to wake up. He slid open the shoji screen of the washroom and peeked through the strong lattice at the courtyard under the pale light. He was overcome by a strange sensation of expectation, or nostalgia, or a teeth-rattling fear. He scanned his eyes from right to left.

Half the body of a miserable-looking figure emerged from the shadow of a lantern and stood there as if spying on him. It was unmistakably Hina. He did not believe this ominous figure with her pale forehead stained by a bit of blood was of this world.

"Oh! Are you Hina? Wait."

He sprung at the storm door beside him and noisily unlocked the sturdy latch used by successful merchants. When he opened one side, he rushed out in a dreamlike state into the courtyard, but all he saw was the stone lantern with an antique clock. Hina was gone like she melted away.

"Hina, what happened?"

His wife Toyo came running out still dressed in her nightclothes. She found her husband slumped down on a garden rock and saw a face that looked bewitched by a fox. Although under waning moonlight, not even a cat could hide in that area.

3

"CAPTAIN, THIS IS THE REASON. This is too much grief for a parent. Death would be better. It's not hard for me to want to hold a funeral."

Oumiya's proprietor Jibei had invited Zenigata Heiji. And he came to learn every detail from around the time of the disappearance of Jibei's daughter to the particulars of the funeral with no deceased.

"My sympathy, sir. As rumored in the world, was this the desire of your daughter's spirit?"

"That's outrageous. My daughter has been seen two or three times, but never spoke a word. The one talking about a funeral without the deceased was that fortuneteller who's always in front of Denpoin Temple."

"All right."

"It was suggested by that bearded fortuneteller Kansouin."

"All right."

"My wife often said, 'If my poor daughter is dead, I want her remains to be found and at least a funeral held.' She wished to have her fortune read by Kansouin. I forbade her. Our daughter's remains flowed out to the coast of the sea, and she would never be seen again by the living. My wife said suffering in the other world is horrible and thought about our pitiful daughter. She wanted her important daily articles and three hundred ryo in gold coins to be placed in a coffin and buried in the family cemetery."

"And that is what happened."

"It can't be helped. We didn't consider that, but if our daughter's afterlife will be serene, that would give us solace," said Jibei and bowed his head. He was a man around forty, despite having the self-assurance of the head of an illustrious family, he seemed sincere but a tad superstitious.

"Don't be shocked, but your daughter is alive."

"What?"

Jibei tossed back his head upon hearing Heiji's unexpected words.

"You may know this, but I rarely go out. I work for the shogun's government but am well acquainted with the miserable business of tying people up. However, when I heard about your daughter's misfortune from my men and rumors floating around town, I could not rest and forced myself to come here."

"..."

"Your daughter is not dead. This is an elaborate swindle. Too many actions are detestable and not normal, so I came. This may sound like boasting, but before three days pass, I will find your daughter."

"Is that true, Captain? If you save my daughter, I would not hesitate to give you half my fortune. If there is any chance she's alive, please save her."

Jibei forgot his dignity as the head of a prosperous house and dropped his hands to the tatami.

"That is unnecessary. Please sit up. I had to come out of selfishness."

"I am well acquainted with the captain's extraordinary temperament. I will tell my wife. She will be elated."

Toyo clapped like she could jump for joy.

"I heard from the next room. Captain, do you believe my daughter is alive?"

Toyo was a woman in her prime older than thirty-six or -seven. One wondered how attractive she was in the past. A little agitated, she clung to Heiji's knee.

"I have suspicions, but please do this for me. If the fortuneteller is keeping shop in front of the gate at Denpoin, I will wash my hands of this case. If the fortuneteller Kansouin hasn't been seen for two or three days, there is no possibility I'm mistaken about your daughter's future being in the hands of some swindler."

These words from Heiji were filled with confidence.

4

WHEN THE SHOP BOY KANEKICHI was sent to the front of the gate at Denpoin, as Heiji predicted, the fortuneteller Kansouin had not been seen for three days. Hina's parents were astonished. They brimmed with the hope that the daughter they believed to be dead may be alive.

"I haven't seen the grave. As a precaution, would you please take me there?"

Zenigata Heiji, Oumiya Jibei, accompanied by a clerk and the construction boss rushed to the temple in Hashiba to look at the grave interring the empty coffin. A clever hoax had occurred, but no suspicious signs of an excavation remained.

"You can rest assured your daughter will be returned unharmed," said Heiji to comfort Jibei and then left for home.

Later on, Oumiya Jibei was irritable and impatient to be reunited with his daughter he had given up for dead but may be alive and well.

"Perhaps, I should put up bulletin boards offering a large reward for the return of Hina. Because I went as far as a funeral with an empty coffin when trapped by a desire, through the power of money, my daughter may be returned."

With parental thoughts and being a wealthy man, in defiance of Heiji's prohibition, he obtained permission from the government office to erect new Missing Person bulletin boards on every important corner in Edo. Naturally, the words and the dimensions of a bulletin board were standard. The writing on the bulletin boards was:

Hina, the daughter of Oumiya Jibei of Hanakawado Pawnbroker and Money Exchange in Edo. 18 years old. When she is returned unharmed to her parents, as thanks, 1,000 ryo will be received.

The rest of the board provided a description of her and other formalities.

Before long, this became the talk of Edo. Within three days, fifty to sixty Hinas appeared. Hina's parents did not see the reality they expected. Their mental preparations and expectations were betrayed. Not one person provided a clue.

Zenigata Heiji was especially dispirited. Today was the third day, but where was she, and how was she hidden? He found no clues to uncover Hina's whereabouts or her kidnappers.

Oumiya Jibei made his living as a pawnbroker and was obstinate in a business where many customers wept. Recently, he achieved wealth, would not take cheap articles, and had no memory of regrets.

Jibei was said to be a good and honest man, and Toyo was reputed to be a beauty when young. She married Jibei twenty years ago and had no relatives nearby; therefore, no rivals in disputes over property were found.

Heiji was at a loss for what to do.

"This is unacceptable. To put a light on where that pretty young woman was hidden, the idea that I would know nothing after three days conflicts with my belief. Well, I'll have to start all over."

From morning on, he only folded his arms and stared at the ornamental potted plants hanging from the eaves.

"Good morning Captain."

Before Heiji spoke, Garappachi opened the clattering door and came in.

"Ah, Garappachi. Has something happened?"

Heiji unfolded his arms but glanced up looking strangely dejected.

"Uh Captain, you're probably a little down about Oumiya, aren't you?"

"If you know that, don't ask unless something has changed."

"Just trying to be civil. If I mentioned some unlucky change, a sensible female dog wouldn't bark at it."

"Are you a fellow having hard times, or is it your usual lack of spending money?"

"As expected, the captain's expert eye hit the target. Since you expected this, can you give me a little loan?"

"You dope. If people saw you, they'd laugh. Hold out your hand. Here take what you need, then go. There's not much."

Heiji took his wallet out of his pocket and pushed it toward Garappachi.

"Thanks so much. This is why the captain is praised. Out in the world, they say Zenigata is skilled, generous, and handsome. That's a big deal."

"Stop with the false flattery."

"Heh, heh. Well, this is enough for today. You don't see a crow with legs bound with a red woman's hair ribbon very much, right?"

"What are you talking about? A crow with its legs bound. Where was that?"

Heiji's attitude suddenly heated up, and with all his strength, he grabbed Garappachi's arms when he picked up the wallet.

"Stuff like that doesn't happen. It's just stupid."

"No, it's something. Where was that crow?"

"Don't be so surprised. Well, a little while ago, some kids caught it at the edge of the seashore and brought it to the guardhouse. Its legs were bound by a ribbon red like a fawn, and a comb was shoved in so the crow couldn't fly away. They grabbed the bird because it was flapping but not flying away. Different from a duck or a pheasant, no one boils and eats a black crow."

"This is serious. Come Garappachi. I must meet and question this crow."

"You're joking?"

Without saying yes or no, Heiji dragged him outside. In the streets of Hanakawado in the early afternoon, the heat soon brought pedestrian traffic to a stop, and the streets were still.

5

THE CROW CAUGHT BY THE CHILDREN remained tied up at the guardhouse. Everyone noisily encircled the wrapped-up bird curious about its surroundings.

"Where are the ribbon and the comb?"

"Captain, come out here. These are the two objects. This isn't someone's strange prank, is it?"

The old watchman brought out a fiery red ribbon and a tortoiseshell comb.

"May I borrow these?" asked Heiji.

"Yes, yes. Take them."

Heiji put the two articles in his pocket but paid no attention to the crow. He hurried to Oumiya.

When he saw Jibei, he asked, "Do you recognize this ribbon and comb?"

"Ah! My daughter wore them in her hair. Where did you find them? With this, you can probably find my daughter. And this...Toyo, Toyo, please come here. The captain has found Hina."

As if holding down the master who became dazed and excited, Heiji said, "Please wait. Your daughter has not been found yet. But I finally have clues in my hands."

Heiji rushed outside.

"I was weak. Now, what will I do?"

On his way home, Garappachi trailed far behind him.

"Captain, have you figured it out?"

A plain-looking face popped up beside him.

"Nope. I know absolutely nothing."

"Really?"

"But Garappachi..."

"Yes."

"No one keeps a crow as a pet."

"Well, that's obvious. A crow doesn't sing or call."

"Be quiet and listen."

"Okay."

"No bird shop anywhere has an example of a crow. Isn't there a pet crow at Doumiya?"

"Yes."

"What do you have to say?"

"Didn't you say to shut up and listen?"

"You are a stubborn guy, but you know where this crow lives?"

"I know in the woods in Okuyama and in Ueno and in Mukojima."

"Fool."

Heiji kept walking in silence.

"There Captain," said Garappachi.

"Ah, you spooked me. What is there?"

"You forgot? The house with the pet crow."

"What, what house with a pet crow? Where?"

"I'll tell you. I'll tell you. It's better if you don't grab my collar."

"A young woman's life is in danger. Do you love your Adam's apple?"

"You scared me."

"You have to stop talking so much nonsense. Where is the house with the pet crow?"

"The haunted mansion recently built in Okuyama."

"What?"

"The crow pecks at the bowels of a drowned body. The drowned body is a doll, but the crow is real. The bird learns about the seeds that have been hidden in a straw mat inserted in the tub. The bird pecks at them like they're loaches. It's amazing, Captain."

"Is that true?"

"It's not true and not a lie. The crow eats too many loaches. Captain, they say that five or six birds are used to replace each other. You often see that sort of trickery."

"Garappachi, I understand. Thank you."

"You're welcome, heh, heh."

For the first time in his life, Garappachi was thanked by Heiji.

"Two people would be conspicuous. You go home and patiently wait."

"Yessir."

"Speak to no one."

Heiji picked up and tucked in his hem and ran at full speed to Okuyama.

6

IN THOSE DAYS, OKUYAMA in Asakusa was a paddy field. Compared to the bustle before the Kaminarimon gate, the scene differed greatly.

Beginning in the spring, a shed was built and surrounded over a wide area by the exhibition of The Haunted Mansion that had been touring the world for a time. The area was desolate. The building was beyond expectations. The exhibition had been popular in Edo since summer began.

Long ago in the Tenpo era, the haunted mansion in Mekichi that evolved from the shed in Higashi Ryogoku and the exhibits of murder victims were popular enough to be chronicled. The haunted mansion in Okuyama was much earlier. The first exhibition showed the ghastly scars on the left sides of the foreheads of Todoroki Gonza and forty or so former ronin. Influential men were among his attendants.

Humans in the forms of dolls, papier-mache, and actual humans were skillfully displayed inside. The handiwork and the planning were meticulous. For the price of admission, Edokko of the day could get as scared as they liked and enjoy gasping in fear at that curious place.

Heiji arrived at the site a little after four in the afternoon precisely at the height of the rush of visitors.

He passed a large signboard of a *Doro-e* painting, paid twenty-four *mon* at the ticket gate and crossed into another world.

The decorations adorning the entrance were a display of dolls against the backdrop of a scene from the kabuki play *Soma no Furugosho*. This was a conventional set-up, but a narrow alley had to be followed to enter the exhibit.

As he passed by the first creation, a one-eyed goblin, under fluttering lantern light, a flying squirrel monster swooped down from above his head and brushed past his face. In the dim light, a monstrous woman with a long wriggling neck seemed to fly out. The legendary bald-headed goblin *Mikoshi-nyudo* glared from a side street. These weren't especially scary, but a huge toad jumped up as he walked the sodden ground. The tail of a giant serpent skimming his forehead unnerved the bug-hating Heiji.

From time to time, curious women entered to squeal and cause a commotion. Although the scenes were ghastly, the frightened women shrieked but did not turn back.

Heiji followed the path equipped with many weapons of attack. After a short time, he was struck by brightness. There was the rumored doll of a drowning victim. In a scene modeled after Okawajiri overgrown with reeds, the bloated body of a drowned woman lay there. Sometimes, a crow flew in with the idea of pecking at her bowels. Heiji understood Garappachi's talk of finding out about seeds and was impressed by this masterful device.

The next room was one side of a cemetery. The stage was dimly lit. Beneath a naturally grown willow tree and in front of white-papered lanterns, a fire fueled by cheap *shochu* alcohol burned. A young woman with disheveled shoulder-length hair and wearing the expected gray unlined kimono with both hands resting on her chest was quickly pushed out from the shadows of the wooden tomb stakes.

This alone would have been an unremarkable idea. However, the figure of the woman who would become a ghost was impressive; and the structure of her face painted with thin black ink over white face powder was expert. This scene was bloodcurdling.

Soon a woman gently advanced holding a bucket and leaned to peek into the well. Without her speaking a word of grievance, the spectators were filled with dread and froze. They all felt as though they were about to be drenched with water.

At that time, no more spectators could enter. Heiji crossed over the green bamboo handrail to step closer to the ghost. For some reason, he suspected she was Hina and got excited.

Surprised by Heiji's behavior, a few spectators backed away to watch. Seeing him, the ghost instantly sunk into the ground like a person falling into a pit. Only the wooden stakes, the white-papered lanterns, the well, and the willow remained in the gloom.

The stunned Heiji returned to the bamboo handrail. The other spectators were gone.

The next room switched to brightness. Scarlet rugs were provided as seats under a pillar tablet stating *Tea will be served.*

The relieved Heiji instinctively looked all around, but no one else was there. Was the approaching sunset to blame? Or was he being shunned because of his earlier behavior? He sat down, absentmindedly crossed his arms, and said, "Tea please."

With eyes cast down, a cute page dressed in a purple large-sleeved kimono, elaborate hakama trousers, and hair styled in two large *chigowa* rings came forward with tea.

"Thank you," said Heiji and picked up the teacup. Heiji was surprised when he looked at the page who had raised his head.

He was a three-eyed goblin.

However, when he realized the third eye had been painted on his forehead, Heiji felt like smiling and looked again at the page's face.

Other than the third eye, his eyes and nose were ordinary. Maybe, this was a girl. The face was very cute.

"Ha, ha. You're a very cute ghost," said Heiji with welcoming eyes.

The small fingers of the page raised the lacquered tray held in his left hand.

"What? What is this?"

Written in proper kana characters was:

> *Captain Zenigata,*
> *Help me. I will meet you tonight at the wooden tomb stakes.*
> *Hina*

"..."

Heiji stared without speaking. The three-eyed goblin was at most twelve or thirteen years old. Because the page was too young to be Hina, perhaps, the page was asked by Hina to write this.

"..."

Heiji nodded.

The bell at Kinryuzan Temple struck exactly six times. The gate was shut, and the ringing echoed from far away.

7

THAT EVENING, ZENIGATA HEIJI slipped in and hid in front of the stage of wooden tomb stakes.

The night grew late. When ten o'clock then midnight passed, the gloomy goblin Mikoshi-nyudo and the huge toad started to move one after the other. This time, he knew they were props and wasn't startled.

In the faint moonlight seeping through the reed screen or rattan blind stretched over the ceiling, Heiji's dark-adapted eyes clearly saw the white-papered lanterns, the willow, and the wooden tomb stakes.

It was soon two in the morning.

Something under the willow tree moved. His night eyes immediately made out a beautiful young woman stretching.

"Oh...Hina-san."

From living in the same town, Heiji knew the familiar face he would recognize even with his eyes shut.

He could see her hair hanging down, her pale face with no make-up, her kimono decorated with autumn colors, and even the red obi sash she wore.

"Sh...Keep quiet, Captain Zenigata. Please show yourself, I—"

"Shh!"

This time Heiji waved his hand to signal someone's approach.

"Hina-san, not yet, try to get away."

When he reached inside for the bamboo handrail…

"Thief! Thief!"

"A thief's in here! Kill him!"

Five or six young men carrying weapons readily spotted and rushed toward Heiji.

"Hey, don't get in the way."

Heiji could not make out his opponents and did not take out his truncheon. He picked up and tossed aside two, but Hina was unable to escape.

"Oh!"

Three more hiding near the tomb stakes flew out…

"Hey, you stubborn witch, this time you die!"

The three converged on her and disappeared with Hina like the ground swallowed them.

In this brawl, Heiji had no choice.

He pushed away and dodged a large man charging at him and entered the darkness behind the props.

"You're not getting away."

The men regrouped to launch another attack, but Heiji had vanished.

8

THE NEXT DAY, THE GATE to the haunted mansion opened as if nothing happened. Lucky or unlucky, that day was a holiday. Visitors poured in from the morning and packed into the narrow haunted lane.

At four in the afternoon, a rumor of unknown origin swiftly spread among the visitors about a special show with a huge prop with a big gimmick. Visitors crammed in during the afternoon and could no longer move. The shed was about to burst open.

"Why hasn't the ghost come out near the wooden tomb stakes?"

"They say today there's gonna be a special show with a big gimmick."

From the wooden tomb stakes near the papier-mache Mikoshi-nyudo, the crowd was tense.

Finally, it was a little before four. At the start of the haunted house performance, Todoroki Gonza appeared dressed in a black silk kimono with a family crest because he hailed from a samurai family and dropped a long tomb stake on the stage of the tomb stakes. The old scar on his forehead was ghastly.

"Today, all of you will witness a special show. This will be a once-in-a-lifetime spectacle. The visitors who enter today will be joyous. All right?"

While speaking his irrelevant monologue, the instant he raised his left hand, a woman appeared from inside the well.

She was a ghost with disheveled hair and dragging a mouse-gray kimono or, maybe, a beautiful seventeen- or eighteen-year-old woman wearing a well-kempt hairstyle of an unmarried woman and light make-up. A red obi sash closed her light-blue kimono. On top, a straw rope went round and round to bind her.

The woman was lifted above the well like a bucket and laid across the well curb.

"Now Ladies and Gentlemen, there is one detail. Please believe I will kill this young woman. There is no trick or device in this sword. The young lady will be hacked to pieces like a fish on this well. Before your eyes will be a very amusing show. A singular event. A once-in-a-lifetime event."

Gonza's words were charged with terrifying authenticity and gnawed at the spectators' hearts. The ones who scoffed at his truth still felt threatened deep in their bowels and held their breath. Others were speechless.

"When she's hacked to pieces, she'll die. Heh, heh, heh. After she dies, she will emerge as a ghost. That is the way. Heh, heh, heh."

The demonic smile covering the cruel shadow in Gonza's cheeks gave the spectators goose bumps. The young woman's eyes were shut, and she could not speak.

"All right. Woman, do you have any final words? You will die a shameful death before everyone. I feel sorrow for your mother's heart."

"Oh, wait!"

The young woman opened her bright eyes. Her faded lips trembled. With just that word, painful cramps ran through her cheeks, and she knitted her sculpted eyebrows.

"Ha, ha, ha. Life is regrettable after all. How sad."

The blade seemed to flash toward the young woman's chest. A single coin caught him off guard.

"Umph!"

It smacked into Gonza's wrist and clanged against the well curb.

"Ow!"

Without thinking, Gonza lowered his sword and tried again with another blade.

"Umph!"

This time, the coin slammed into Gonza's forehead near the old scar. Of course, the flying coin was the special talent of Zenigata Heiji.

"Ow!"

Blood trickled down.

"Todoroki Gonza! You are under arrest!"

When the papier-mache Mikoshi-no-nyudo tipped over, Heiji jumped out from inside and scrambled over the shoulders of the dazed crowd to fly over the bamboo handrail.

"You're under arrest!"

"Come quietly."

Four or five of his men emerged from the crowd to follow Heiji and swooped down on the area of the tomb stakes to surround Gonza.

HINA WAS RESCUED UNHARMED.

Todoroku Gonza had been a former lover of her mother Toyo, but he misbehaved and she gave up on him. He resented Toyo's marriage soon after to the wealthy Jibei. Twenty years later, he kidnapped her only daughter Hina. He had a thought more horrible than the deaths of Toyo and her husband. He ignored the one-thousand-ryo reward of gold and patiently bided his time. He waited for the opportunity to dispel his terrifying viper-like resentment.

He spotted Zenigata Heiji's intrusion and realized his defeat was near. He told the three-eyed goblin to lure in Heiji so he could kill him with Hina, but Heiji was not hiding by the papier-mache Onyudo monster. In desperation, the following day he planned to stab Hina at the well in the cemetery near the tomb stakes to be witnessed by many spectators. This end would bring him satisfaction.

The fortuneteller Kansouin was Gonza's man. And it was Hina who tied the crow's legs with the red ribbon and set it free.

Sergeant Sasano Shinsaburo said, "Heiji, did you fail this time?"

"Yes, Gonza is beyond redemption. He's a detestable fellow," answered Heiji cheerfully but was distressed by handing a man over at the prison gate. His brow knitted, but there was nothing he could do.

CHAPTER SIX

THE SHAPE OF
A VENGEFUL DEMON

1

"HELP! HELP ME PLEASE!"

The footman Yukichi ran up the steps at the entrance glancing all around.

He was at the official government-provided residence of the Hatchobori Police Sergeant Sasano Shinsaburo. On that day, the master Shinsaburo attended a crucifixion at Suzugamori, but settling the affair was delayed and he had not returned home. His wife Kuni accompanied by a few attendants had been invited to her family home in Hamacho to enjoy the river festival in Ryogoku and hadn't returned home either.

Recently, when the master and the mistress were absent, Shizu, Zenigata Heiji's fiancee, would leave her job at a roadside teahouse in Ryogoku, and come to learn good manners through an apprenticeship at this upper-class home from the elderly steward Odashima Denzo. Kichi, an attractive woman approaching middle age and a distant relative of the master Shinsaburo, five or six maidservants and garden sweepers were quietly waiting for the master and mistress to return.

The commotion occurred at that time.

"What's going on...?"

When they rushed out to look, Yukichi was squatting at the entrance and carrying piggyback Shinsaburo's only child, the five-year-old Shintaro, who was also looking around.

"Oh, the young master."

"What happened?"

Shintaro, a child of nobility, was as cute as a doll and was dressed in luxurious silk gauze. He was taken in arms amid calls for a doctor and medicine. Fortunately, he soon regained his energy, but the sight was frightening. He had been sobbing, shivering, and unable to speak.

While looking around, the attendant Yukichi placed Shintaro down on the wood floor of the entrance for convenience, and he began to come around. However, Yukichi thought this shameful and was about to sneak away, but the old man Odashima called him from behind.

"Hold on there, Yukichi."

"Yes, yes."

"What are you doing? While caring for the important young master, you're looking all around like a coward."

"Yes."

"First of all, what is this? You returned alone before the others. What happened to the lady? Tell me."

In the old way of thinking, that was unpardonable.

"Yes."

Yukichi was an amiable young man of twenty-five or -six years old. He looked wise and strong, but by some twist of fate, he was a born coward.

He was a hanger-on always being teased by friends with words like "Is this because Yukichi's a big coward?"

"This is not the place for doubts. What happened? Did he bite you? Can't you speak?"

"Yes. I'm sorry. I lost sight of the lady and the maid in the crowds in Ryogoku. So I got ready to go home, and with the young master on my back, I came back to Hamacho without telling anyone."

"Hmm."

"Well, everyone has gathered in Ryogoku, so there was none of that Edo loneliness tonight."

"You dope."

"There wasn't a soul anywhere. I returned while chatting with the young master on my back. But all of a sudden, on a street in Ningyocho, I was confronted by a man and wondered what was going on. I shivered at what I saw."

"Get a hold of yourself. Don't talk like a dope because you're a fine young man."

"It was...that case."

"What do you mean by that case?"

"A bloodied man carrying a crucifixion cross on his back—"

"What?"

"That guy who murdered his master was crucified today in Suzugamori."

"Something that stupid happens?"

"Stupid or not, you'll see if you ask the young master. He ran by in a flash like he was chasing someone with a vengeance. I ran from Ningyocho to Hatchobori, when I reached the entrance to the mansion, my mind relaxed, and I collapsed. Is there a bloodied guy carrying a cross on his back near the gate? Please look out for me."

With teeth-chattering fear, Yukichi took all his strength to reason this far in his story.

"Was that here? You dope. Pull yourself together. It's all the fault of your cowardice."

The old man Odashima was not against him.

"You say that, but please give me a little credit because I struggled back here without falling down along the way. I thought about the precious young master on my back and panicked. Didn't I do right?"

"Don't brag so much or you'll pass out. A damn fool. It'll be unforgivable if the young master is sick."

"Yes."

In the midst of the furor, the master Sasano Shinsaburo and his wife Kuni returned home.

2

A MYSTERIOUS CURSE CAST on the family of Sergeant Sasano Shinsaburo began with repeated vengeful acts.

With the night came insects, his son Shintaro slept poorly some evenings. His young mother Kuni was beside herself with worry.

One evening, Shintaro was finally lulled to sleep. When Kuni neared the storm shutter, an object was brightly lit by the last rays of moonlight shining on the window shoji screen, which was usually left open until late at night.

She looked again and recognized a freshly severed human head.

"Oh!" she gasped.

However, the wife in a samurai family is taught discretion from birth and, more importantly, not to cause a scene.

She gently slid out along the floor and went to the adjoining room to nudge Shinsaburo awake.

"Husband, please, there is something I wish you to see," she whispered.

"What? Has a burglar snuck in?"

With his sword in hand and still in his nightclothes, Shinsaburo went to investigate. He looked where Kuni pointed and jumped back.

The topknot of the severed head was tangled in the window grating causing the head to dangle down from the window lattice fully lit by the late moon.

"Hmm,"

Shintaro moaned once. Shinsaburo hesitated, but in the next moment, he grabbed and opened the screen.

Moonlight flowed in like water.

The pale blue light hit half his face. Lashed to the window grating was a bloody severed head of a middle-aged man. The wide-open, two unseeing eyes and the white teeth biting the lower lip created a gruesome expression of spite.

"Ah!"

Surprised, Kuni sunk down like she fainted. Shintaro, who had just fallen asleep, began crying as if set on fire.

The face of this head had been seared vividly in Sasano Shinsaburo's memory. That unforgettable face on the head chopped off that day at the Suzugamori execution grounds belonged to a man who struggled to cling to life. The head belonging to a counterfeiter was the most unsightly and most gruesome in its last moments.

The subsequent series of unfortunate events mysteriously occurred only on execution days. While avoiding the investigating police sergeant Sasano Shinsaburo, severed heads and corpses appeared as unrelenting, repeated threats.

The staff was expanded to conduct a strict night patrol, but, in the end, no clues were discovered. When unable to enter the grounds, he threw the unclean objects stolen from the execution grounds into the garden from outside the fence and made a hasty escape.

"Husband, please do something. By throwing and leaving those abominations here, your rival has grown impudent. We have no idea what he's capable of doing."

Kuni sometimes spoke in this way to encourage her husband's determination. But, what was Shinsaburo thinking? The days multiplied when he was unable to listen, nodded at her, and used few words.

3

AT A LOSS, WHEN SHINSABURO was away from home, Kuni called Ishihara Risuke for a consultation.

Kuni was a woman in her prime at twenty-six years old and lacked neither beauty nor wisdom. Her son's condition showed no progress, and the unearthly events continued. She could no longer bear it. She said, "Risuke, here is the reason. Taking into consideration my husband's office, it would be awful if this matter became known to the world. Please do your best to prevent that from happening."

"Yes, ma'am. I understand. I am sorry for so many phantoms playing with idiotic threats, but through my observant black eyes, I will shrink them down to one."

Risuke swallowed hard and wiped his slightly glistening forehead. Similar to Zenigata Heiji, he was a detective with the favor of Sasano Shinsaburo, but lately, the reputation of the young Heiji was outstanding. Kuni initiated this consultation with a man who was a bit exasperated and found this to be a timely offer.

Risuke said, "Of course, there must be an accomplice inside. That kind of clever trick would be impossible from the outside. Please describe everyone who lives in the mansion."

"In addition to my husband, son, and me, there is a relative named Kichi, a distant relative of my husband. She is my age, twenty-six, and pretty. You may not have met her."

"No, I know about her. Her parents died, and there was talk about her marrying your husband. However, that idea was abandoned, and she became a dependent of your household."

"You know quite a lot."

"Heh, heh. It's only business. I'm shrewd in those matters."

"That is unsettling."

"Any suspicions would first fall on that person. Who would you say held a grudge against your husband and you? If anyone felt spiteful, she would have the best reason to harbor a grudge against people in this mansion."

"That's true. You could say that, but Kichi-san is truly a fine woman."

"People who commit heinous acts have exceptional human touch. Who else is there?"

"There are the servants. First, the steward is Odashima-san."

"That man has no connection with monsters."

"The footman Yukichi."

"That coward?"

"And Heiji's bride-to-be Shizu."

"Hmm."

Kuni named all the employees. Nonetheless, Ishihara Risuke was only interested in Kichi.

"Would you please call Kichi-san?"

"If I do, my husband will know immediately."

"That's all right. If I can't use my menacing look, she will become brazen, and I will never unravel this situation. And didn't your husband leave on a trip to his domain in Shimousa?"

"The caretaker of his inherited estate has fallen ill. My husband went to act as the agent and will not return for four or five days."

"Isn't that fortunate? As they say, when the cat's away... If evidence emerges during that time, I will grab onto it."

Risuke was a little too eager for success in everything accomplished by the young Heiji. Despite seeming wise, Kuni felt a trace of jealousy toward Kichi, who was rumored to have received a proposal from her husband Shinsaburo. In the end, however, they came to an agreement about this serious situation.

4

AT A GUARDED LOCATION INSIDE the mansion, rat poison from the Iwami Silver Mines had been placed in Shintaro's bowl of side dishes. Fortunately, the child was saved because he hated the smell and refused to eat the dish. If not, the result would have been unbearable.

Kuni was enraged and summoned Ishihara Risuke for a consultation. While her husband Shinsaburo was away, Kichi would be confined to one room. In a polite but firm tone, Risuke reproached Kichi.

He said, "Kichi-san, I don't want to speak about this matter, but the handiwork is too clever. Without someone like you present, the performance would have been impossible. Your grudge is against the master and the lady. Are you a woman who would threaten the innocent young master and use rat poison to rob him of his life?"

"What are you saying? I am truly appalled," she said.

"Don't play innocent. If you don't tell me now, I have no choice but to take you before a court of law. I ask you kindly to surrender for your sake."

"What are you saying? Are you accusing me of committing those unearthly acts of evil?"

As a dependent and a servant, the well-raised Kichi had been caught by the astute detective and could barely speak. She was flustered and snagged by the trap strung by Risuke, and had no idea what would happen next.

He said, "You don't look kindly on the good relationship between the master and the lady."

She said, "Although I am human, I will serve you because I have now given up on everything."

"Well said. You are quite glib. Are people taken in by your words? Anyway, I cannot let you out to roam free and cause trouble. You will be confined until the master returns. Can you endure this? I will attend to you, so you won't be lonely."

Finally, Risuke threw Kichi in the storeroom and watched her like a hawk.

Shizu, who was Kichi's best friend, was the person most surprised.

Even if the usually prudent and slightly timid Kichi became giddy with jealousy, she would never think of committing such a heinous act. Although they considered speaking up for Kichi, the servants sadly did not have the status to reproach the lady. Also, in front of the storeroom holding Kichi, the smart police detective, who had a tinge of the eeriness of his occupation, would glower at a mouse passing by.

The one who unexpectedly came to the place of reflection was Shizu's fiance, Zenigata Heiji.

Shinsaburo had not yet returned from Shimousa, but there was work to do. When Heiji went inside to say hello and went down to the kitchen, his usual adversary Risuke was sitting on a cushion in front of the closed door of the storeroom and blowing smoke rings from a cheap cigarette with an air of importance.

"Ah, Ishihara-san, what's going on?"

"Zenigata? It's been a while."

"Yes, we haven't crossed paths in a long time. What are you doing here?"

"What? Nothing at all."

"..."

This situation was peculiar. The quick-thinking Heiji took note of the details and instead of pressing the issue, he chatted about the weather and then left.

He was about to go out the kitchen door to the streets of Hatchobori when he heard, "Wait a moment, please, Captain."

Shizu was coming toward him and slightly out of breath. She had shown only her face a little while ago in the kitchen.

"What is it Oshi darling? Is there someone here you call Captain?"

"I'm not sure what I should call you."

"Well, let's see. You can't call me dear, but anything would be nice."

"What?!"

"Enough of that. What's the matter? It's probably not a plan to show me a pretty place. It's probably the matter of Ishihara encamped in front of the storeroom."

"Yes, that's it. Something horrible has happened. Poor Kichi-san. The poor thing."

"Why do you suddenly look like you're about to cry? Why don't you tell me everything from the beginning."

Zenigata Heiji, the famous catcher of criminals, and Shizu, whose beauty echoed throughout Ryogoku at the time, entered the shadows on the street to avoid the eyes of others and the sunshine.

5

NEXT, ZENIGATA HEIJI COLLUDED with Shizu on a last-ditch effort. If the worst happened while they idly waited for the return of the master Shinsaburo, an incident might unfold and permanently stain the extraordinarily favored Sasano family.

Ishihara Risuke focused on Kichi as the villain and browbeat her to force a confession by any means to name her accomplice outside the mansion. However, Kichi was stubborn, sealed her mouth, and only looked down. Ishihara Risuke felt torture was his only option, but after two or three days, it became too much for him.

On the other hand, during this time, Heiji set out to investigate the servants. The elderly Odashima Denzo worked there for over thirty years. Most of the servants had been working there for five to ten years. The shortest time was a little over one year. Heiji did not think any of them held a grudge against the master.

Heiji thought about the cases of awful acts and the severity of the punishments. He conducted various investigations such as whether people had been subjected to unreasonable punishment in cases handled by Sasano Shinsaburo over the past three years. Sasano Shinsaburo was a famous police sergeant at the time and held a grim temporary post. Some people felt his decisions were too lenient; therefore, Heiji did not believe there was a reason to resent him.

As Heiji's investigation made slow progress, another horrible incident occurred.

Recently, Shintaro had been safe and sound, and allowed to go out to play with Shizu in the garden and go as far as the gate. The incident began when he asked to go to the festival day at Suiten-gu Shrine.

Kuni had no idea what to do and consulted with Risuke. He had no objections because Kichi, who tormented Shintaro, had been taught a lesson. And he could not stop his opponent, a mother who spoiled her son.

As a precaution, Yukichi went along with Shizu. About two hours later, the day grew dark and Yukichi was alone.

"Maybe, the young master and Shizu-san went home?"

With a carefree look on his face, he returned home in no hurry.

"What happened to my son and Shizu?" asked the surprised Kuni as she flew outside.

Yukichi said matter-of-factly, "Shizu-san met an acquaintance and they went into a roadside teahouse on the grounds, but never came out after a long time had passed. I thought she left by the back door and went home."

"What?!" she said and sent everyone out to search everywhere. However, Shintaro and Shizu were nowhere to be found.

When inquiries were made at the teahouse, no one had noticed them in the crowd. Everyone they asked whether in Shizu's neighborhood or near Heiji's home had no idea. In a remarkable disappearance, the two vanished like smoke from the grounds of the Suiten-gu Shrine.

The frantic Kuni said, "I will offer a reward for the desired outcome to those looking for my son."

She was at a loss for what to do if this were a clever kidnapping.

In the mayhem, a maid came carrying a strange object.

She held it out and said, "A little while ago, someone tossed this through the kitchen door."

The object was a hastily prepared wishing paper attached to a strip of bamboo.

"Let's see what this is," said Risuke as he took it. The note was just three lines written in coarse kana characters.

> If you don't want Shintaro to die,
> free Kichi.
> She is innocent.

"Dammit. This one is cocky. This is a scheme for her accomplice outside to save her."

Risuke stamped his foot in frustration and regret.

Kuni said weakly in a motherly tone, "If there's a chance of saving my son... I may regret it, but let that woman out of the storeroom and let her go wherever she wants."

Risuke grew a backbone and would not listen. He said, "Madam, that is absurd. He didn't say the young master would be returned when she is freed. Clearly, the woman must appear in a court of law. If she speaks, everything will become clear."

"Oh, we'll do as you say. I don't know what is happening," said Kuni, who was exhausted and could only shed bitter tears.

Risuke said, "Very well. I will show no mercy. Woman, come here."

He opened the storeroom door and dragged out Kichi weakened by over three days of confinement.

"What are you going to do?" she asked.

"Shut up. Come and you'll see. If that's not agreeable to you, tell me the name of your accomplice and his hideout."

Kichi let out a pitiful cry as she was wrenched down to the ground and her arms pulled behind her and quickly bound.

"It will be a problem if you fight. Walk!"

He cruelly yanked the rope.

"Ow, ow," Kichi cried as she fell against the wall of the narrow veranda.

6

RIGHT AFTER RISUKE LED KICHI away, Heiji came flying in.

"The young master is missing? What? He was kidnapped from Suitengu?"

He went inside through the kitchen and said, "Madam, this is awful. You must be terribly worried."

At a time like this, the usually subdued Heiji could not restrain himself. He spoke from outside the door to ask how Kuni was feeling.

In her confusion, she forgot her usual reserve and said, "Oh Heiji, thank goodness you came. Please save the young master. I beg you."

He asked, "Where is Ishihara-san?"

"He tied up Kichi-san and took her to the magistrate to make her confess about her accomplice."

"What? He did something that lawless..."

"If he didn't, that woman would not confess."

"That's ridiculous. Kichi-san doesn't understand, but what was he thinking when he led a criminal from the home of the police sergeant?"

"What?"

"At the very least, the sergeant may be fired. At worst, he may lose his stipend. The master cannot escape the crime of mismanagement of household matters."

"Oh goodness!"

"Even if that doesn't happen, the government officials who thought of him as a shrewd young master and an ally may be greatly disappointed. This has become absurd."

This was Heiji's fear. Sasano Shinsaburo may have made formidable enemies in his office as an investigating police sergeant and had no reason to be calm about a criminal being taken from his home.

It was not unreasonable for Kuni as a woman to be unaware of this. However, Ishihara Risuke was fully aware. Unless they were out of sight in the early evening, why was a criminal pulled through the gate of the police sergeant's house and deliberately taken to the magistrate?

"This was not a matter of life and death to the young lord. A more important matter was a criminal matter capable of staining the household. Around what time did Risuke leave?"

"He just left."

Kuni felt ashamed and was unable to look up.

"That may not be the outcome, but I should pursue them. Excuse me."

Heiji slipped out through the kitchen and dashed to the magistrate in Minami-cho in Sukiyabashi.

7

WHEN HEIJI REACHED SANJIKKENHORI River in the evening twilight, he saw the figures of a man and a woman hurrying to the other side.

He called out, "Ishihara, wait there please."

Heiji ran up to them as fast as a flying bird and blocked their way.

"What is it, Heiji? What do you want?" asked Ishihara Risuke glaring at him.

Heiji said, "Kichi-san doesn't know anything. It's pitiful. Will you untie the rope and give her to me?"

"What are you talking about? She has proof. Doesn't the law allow me to carry a truncheon and a rope and to make arrests?" asked Risuke.

"It's not that. You took a criminal from the mansion of Sergeant Sasano. Words cannot express how indebted we are to the master. If she has some sort of evidence, you don't want to force Kichi-san to confess before the court and destroy Master Sasano. Do you understand, Ishihara?

Because I am asking you, please untie her and hand her over. I'll hunt down the rogue and evil kidnapper, and you will have the credit and success."

Risuke said, "What? What are you saying? Be quiet and listen. Why do you talk like I'm a rookie and you'll catch the bad guy and give me the credit? You're afraid because I have ten years more experience than you as a detective. Go home. Get out of here. Admit defeat and go away. Just leave."

"Is that all you can say, Risuke?"

"I'll say it loud and clear. This woman has become important lately. Are you going to snatch her away?"

"What? Won't you listen to reason? It's for the sake of Sergeant Sasano."

Heiji pulled the rope binding Kichi and quickly began to untie it.

"What are you doing?"

Risuke acted disgracefully and grabbed at Heiji.

"Risuke, this is inexcusable," said Heiji, then turned and with all his might pushed Risuke from behind. This sent him headlong into a ditch on the side of the road.

"Ah!"

Heiji looked with contempt at Risuke and said, "I'll apologize later. Try to understand."

Heiji urged Kichi to go back down the road. They returned as fast as they could.

8

AFTER HEIJI FOLLOWED RISUKE and ran off with Kichi, Sasano Shinsaburo returned from Shimousa. Did he have a premonition? Strangely, he returned because of homesickness. Right at that time, a courier had been dispatched to the estate in Shimousa. The entire mansion was in an uproar.

As Kuni and the servants told him various details and his shock grew, Yukichi, who lazily returned home from Suiten-gu a while ago, appeared unexpectedly at the garden gate and made a strange statement, "Master, I just remembered. I remember the man who invited Kichi to the teahouse at Suiten-gu."

"Why have you been silent until now? Who? Who was that man?" asked Shinsaburo.

"I forgot all about him. Well, I don't know his name, but I've seen him in Ochanomizu."

"Do you know where he lives?"

"If I go and look, I can probably find it."

"Very good. Take me there."

Shinsaburo wanted to fly there and, still in his traveling clothes, he called two palanquins, and they charged at full speed to Ochanomizu.

When they arrived at Shohei-bashi Bridge, the guide Yukichi unexpectedly said, "We'll get out here and walk. It wouldn't be good to go by palanquin."

No longer needed, the palanquins went home, and Yukichi guided Shinsaburo. They slowly climbed up to the front of a shrine and walked toward Ochanomizu. In those days, there was no bridge, but at a location with a good view, a couple of teahouses sat on a cliff thirty or forty feet high. Excuse the digression, but one story passed down says that at this place, the painter Hasegawa Settan, who later drew and painted famous sites of Edo, was mistaken for a traitor as he sketched this scene of the teahouses.

Beside the road at the location of the teahouse, a famous cooling hut with reed screens and a coarse shingled roof over footholds was built to overhang the cliff at Ochanomizu. At noon, there were several customers, but at dusk, the shops quickly closed. Old and young women were going home with their boxes of candy and scarlet carpets on their backs, and large teakettles dangling down.

Understandably, the area from the front of the shrine to Motomachi was desolate. Because of the Matsudaira Skinning Incident during the shogunate era until the onset of the Meiji era, this became a favorite haunt for bandits and for killing a passerby to test one's sword.

The coward Yukichi briskly entered, but Sasano Shinsaburo held back a little.

However, when the consequences would affect the life and death of his only child Shintaro, it was not the time for too many questions. He followed in silence. Yukichi entered the teahouse furthest away of the three buildings on the cliff and opened the door of a building that had been deteriorating for a long time.

"He's in here, master," said Yukichi and escorted him inside.

"Did you say Shintaro is here?"

"Yes, he's definitely here. Please wait a moment while I get a light."

Yukichi invited Shinsaburo in and went back out.

Shinsaburo waited for a while, but Yukichi didn't return. In the grim darkness, he couldn't see an inch in front of him. He could hear the soft sounds of water below the floorboards on the cliff thirty or forty feet high.

"What's going on?"

Shinsaburo stood still. He trusted the honest Yukichi but felt uneasy. When he tried to grope his way back to the door, he wondered had nails been removed from the floorboards, or a trap been set? A board under his foot sprung back, and he screamed, "Eeeyaah!"

Shinsaburo's body was no longer supported and dropped down several dozen feet.

9

"HEH, HEH, ARE YOU FINALLY gonna fall?"

A voice came out of the darkness.

He heard the sound of a sickle striking a flint, and the room was brightened by a candle.

In the light, Shinsaburo saw his footman Yukichi, the man he only thought of, until that moment, as a coward. Yukichi's face was queerly tense and holding a candle to inspect the hole Shinsaburo fell into.

"Hey, Yugoro."

"Yukichi?" asked a voice from far below.

"Dammit, what happened?"

"He didn't fall."

"That can happen?"

"If he falls, we should hear a thud. If there's the slightest chance he crawls to the shore from the boat, I'll be waiting there and skewer him with a bamboo spear. He'll never say a word."

"What should I do?"

Yukichi thrust the candle he held in his left hand through the hole and looked down.

"Ah, he's up here. Right there."

"Look there!"

Shinsaburo was gripping a thick hemp rope hanging from a sturdy crossbeam below the floor. Nearly in the center, Shintaro and Shizu were bound hand and foot and gagged. Almost a third of the way from the top of the rope was another person dangling down.

He was Sasano Shinsaburo, who fortunately found the rope and feverishly grabbed it after falling through the hole. Because the palms of his hands were skinned by the force of his falling body, he could not pull himself up the rope.

While he clenched his teeth and barely supported his body, in the light of the candle shining from above, the coward Yukichi saw that Shinsaburo had fallen through and was on the edge of death, and he saw the boat below him.

When Shinsaburo struggled to contort his body in order to see Yukichi's face, his eyes first caught the contemptible sight of his son Shinsaburo and Shizu tied to the same rope dangling in the space below his feet, and not the villain in the boat.

"Oh, Shintaro! And Shizu!" he said but was powerless to act.

Above him, Yukichi quickly saw them and said, "Master, did you see them? Fate is for the father and son, and the master and servant to die together. Heh, heh, you should probably give up."

He bared his teeth in hate.

"Yukichi, what is the meaning of this? You were supposed to take care of them, but your grievance led you to carry out this cruel act. Your grievance is against me, but why do you condemn the innocent Shintaro and Shizu to this cruelty?"

Shinsaburo thought he would spit blood. He was losing strength in his hands that barely supported his body and glared with indignant eyes.

Yukichi said, "You still don't get it? My older brother who's on the boat down there was forced to carry the crucifixion cross. To scare that brat, I took a severed head from Suzugamori and hung it outside his window. I did everything to get our revenge. You probably didn't notice because your circulation is bad. What are we hiding? For the crime of using measuring boxes with forged official seals, the heads of the rice dealer Echigoya Yusuke and his wife were displayed at the execution grounds three years ago. We are their orphans."

"What?!"

"A corrupt clerk provided those items himself. His fattening his own pocket burdened our parents who knew nothing. The crime of fake measuring boxes is serious. We'll never forget the sight of their gray-haired heads lined up outside in Suzugamori. It was all your doing. Our hatred of the world grew. This teahouse was bought with the secret savings of our mother who perished. The two of us wandered the world lost and half-starved for a long time. We only wanted to strike at our enemy. We looked for a way to get close to you, and me, as the younger brother, entered service at your home."

"..."

"The criminal clerk, who provided the fake measuring boxes, disappeared. So it made sense to direct our rage at you Sergeant Sasano Shinsaburo, the man who arrested our parents."

"..."

"My brother Yugoro is down there. No one is gonna climb up that rope and lower them down to safety. How long will their torment last before they die? At that time, we'll speak final words for their departed souls. Watch!"

"..."

"Yugoro, they're coming down. Watch out."

"Okay. Hold them in the air and I'll spear them."

Yukichi started to cut the rope with his short sword.

He repeatedly struck the sword against the strong rope of three twisted strands.

"That's one," he said when one strand broke. The rope strands spun and the three bodies turned in space.

10

"ANOTHER ONE CUT."

In desperation, Shinsaburo said, "Wait, wait, Yukichi. Your grudge is misdirected, despite what you've said, stop what you're doing. I'll surrender and let you kill me. My son and Shizu committed no crime. I'll swing out and drop into the river. Please don't cut the rope, pull them up and save those two. I beg you, Yukichi."

Shinsaburo slightly raised up the bodies hanging below him. In the red firelight of the candle, the resentment etched on Yukichi's face did not soften.

"Hey, Yugoro what are we gonna do?"

"There's only one choice. We're doing this for our parents. Quick, finish cutting."

"Okay."

The sword cut the second strand.

"Just one more. Say your prayers," said Yukichi in a poisonous tone.

"Shintaro, Shizu, this is awful, but you heard what he said. Reconcile yourselves, we will die together," said Shinsaburo looking down at peace with his fate.

"Good, you're ready," said Yukichi placing his sword on the last strand.

"Amen!"

An instant later, a single coin soared in.

The coin slammed into Yukichi's palm and made the hand holding the short sword tremble.

"Stop! Stop!" said Zenigata Heiji as he leaped from the darkness.

"Huh? Stay out of the way."

Heiji and Yukichi scuffled for a time. The short sword swung up and down and was finally knocked out of Yukichi's hand. Heiji seemed to possess superior strength. He pushed Yukichi and grabbed and held him up like a kitten.

"It's over!"

A loud splash came after Yukichi was thrown forty feet down into the currents of Ochanomizu at night.

THESE EVENTS UNFOLDED BECAUSE Heiji rushed into a perilous situation.

Heiji beat up Risuke in Sanjikkenhori and took him back to Hatchobori. When he heard Shinsaburo had been lured away by Yukichi, he understood as if the secret of this case were reflected in a mirror.

When Heiji heard various facts from Shizu, his intuition told him this was the work of a resentful servant. Before three days passed, he conducted a thorough undercover investigation of the identities of all of the servants. He discovered that the footman Yukichi was the son of the executed Echigoya and located the run-down teahouse in Ochanomizu.

When Heiji heard Yukichi mentioned the Ochanomizu area, he solved this case. He worked the palanquin and his legs to their limits and arrived in time at the moment of danger.

Shinsaburo gathered all his power to raise Shintaro and Shizu with him to the floor of the teahouse.

He said, "Arrest Yukichi and Yugoro!"

As Heiji's eyes scanned the waters on the dark night, he said unconcerned, "Maybe they're dead. Let them go. It's tragic they were convinced a false charge led to their parents' deaths. However, those brothers will not repeat this evil act."

CHAPTER SEVEN

THE CASE OF OSAN'S TATTOO

1

"HEY, GARAPPACHI!"

"Garappachi is bad for my reputation. Could you please try to call me Hachi or Hachiko?"

"Stop being so grand. But when a beautiful young courtesan is nearby, I'll call you, Hachi-san or Hachi. Most of the time, the normal Garappachi is good enough. Don't get full of yourself."

"I'm stuck with a miserable nickname. At least, I'm the right-hand man of Captain Zenigata Heiji. How about calling me Koban Gold Hachigoro?"

"You dope. Everyone would laugh. Why don't you go out to the street and strike a pose?"

"Huh?"

The famous lawman Zenigata Heiji and his sidekick Garappachi carried on this useless exchange as they walked along the Hamacho shore to Ryogoku.

Whenever they met, they only talked nonsense, but the pair made a strangely congenial boss and follower. For an intelligent police detective like Heiji, the not-too-bright but honest Garappachi who spared no pains to do his job was a perfect fit as his sidekick.

"But Hachi."

"Ah, thank you for dropping the *Gara*. What is it, Captain?"

"You probably know where we're going today."

"No, I don't. When the captain suddenly says, 'Come on let's go,' I just follow. Because time is time, and maybe I'll get a treat of food or drink even if I have to wear myself out."

"You are a dope and always thinking about getting fed. You're not so sharp today."

"In that case, how long before I can eat and drink again? How many *ri* can people walk? Will it be like you're giving me a test?"

"No, it's not a serious crime. I have a strange question for you. Have you dirtied your body?"

"Dirtied my body?"

"I mean do you have a tattoo? The truth is a meeting's being held today at Tanemura in Ryogoku called *The Tattoo Pride Conference*."

"Huh?"

"I thought I'd go and see. Even a tattoo no bigger than a fleabite is fine. You see, you can't go in without a tattoo."

"Okay, I'll be okay."

"Do you have one?"

"It's sorry looking, but look here," said Garappachi and rolled up the hem of his kimono. On the ankle of his left leg, a line drawing of a small peach seed was tattooed.

"Ha, ha. That tattoo is pitiful."

"It's like you say. It looks like the tracks of fleabites. You say that, Captain, but have you dirtied your body?"

"I have, but you must not copy it."

"Captain, I've washed your back several times and never noticed a tattoo."

"Well, you weren't paying attention, because there is one."

"Let me have a look?"

"Am I supposed to strip in the street? I'm not a footman or a fireman."

"If I don't see it, I won't have peace of mind. If you go to that meeting, only you, Captain Zenigata, will be attacked at the gate. That will be my shame."

"You worry too much."

While they talked nonsense, they arrived at the entrance to Tanemura, the largest restaurant in the district located behind the bridge guard and the expansive archery grounds in Ryogoku.

"Welcome."

"Captain Zenigata has come."

"'Scuse me," said Heiji in a loud voice and his eyes half open as he passed inside. Four or five organizers were in front of Tanemura and pulled on the strange haori coats to inspect the body of each person entering and leaving. Instead of money, they looked for the presence or absence of a tattoo. However, Heiji's face was widely known. Foregoing the rude exposure of his skin, he passed through the gate and was escorted inside.

In a hall facing the river and stretching three or four rooms, five or six men proud of their tattoos had already gathered. Heiji did not single out a particular face among them.

"Captain, Ishihara's here," said Garappachi while tugging on Heiji's sleeve. He scolded Garappachi with his eyes and quietly retreated to a corner.

2

TATTOOS ARE SAID TO HAVE originated in the tattooing of criminals and barbarians tattooing themselves to threaten ferocious beasts. After the Genroku era (1688–1704), this practice thrived and the advances in technique accelerated particularly during Houreki (1751–1764), Meiwa (1764–1772), and Kansei (1789–1801). From the Kan'ei era (1624–1644) to Meireki (1655–1658), during Heiji's time, the practice was of little importance.

As is seen from the patterns, advances in large-pattern tattoos were reflected in advances in kabuki plays and in ukiyo-e art. The word *kurikaramonmon*, which remains today to indicate large elaborate tattoos, was brought to Edo by the kabuki performer Nakamura Utaemon III, who had tattoos covering both arms, and entered usage after his performance in the role of Kurikara Taro.

In the age of this story, simple tattoos resembling characters and patterns advanced into pictures, but were not yet the elaborate patterns in the ukiyo-e style with large designs and shading. However, when these rare, curious people in the world flourished and held this type of gathering, naturally, people proud of their tattoos throughout Edo and those having tattoos resembling a track of fleabites all flocked to the meeting partly to sightsee.

Ninety-eight people gathered after the appointed time of two o'clock in the afternoon until four o'clock. They all drew lots and then in numerical order, they exposed their skin for all to see. First, a young man, who looked like a fireman, had the faces of an ugly man tattooed on his chest and a homely woman on his back. The people of that time were amazed and praised him because the worked looked naive and intricate.

The next man to come out was middle-aged, perhaps in his thirties.

"Please excuse me," he said defiantly and showed a frog and a slug tattooed on his buttocks and a small snake coiled above the three sections of his loincloth.

The third to come out had a gourd on a branch of a cherry tree tattooed on his back. This tattoo was not intricate like those that appeared after the restrictive Kansei and Tenpo Reforms but dazzled the eyes of those present.

Thus, all ninety-eight participants stripped naked and were graded by the organizers. The plan was to award the prizes of a sack of polished rice for first place and a roll of fabric for second place. After that era, once in Bunka year 8 (1811) and once during the Tenpo Reforms (1842–1845), tattoos were strictly forbidden by law. However, competitions of this form were frequently sponsored until the recent Restoration; therefore, few, if any, older people have recollections of these events.

The peach on Garappachi's ankle was too shabby. But Zenigata Heiji's tattoo was mysteriously fitting. When he stripped, six coins (three coins across and two down), like the crest of the Sanada clan, were tattooed in the center of his back.

Finally, all ninety-eight people were naked. On this day, first prize was a competition between a gambler with the marriage of the fox tattooed over his entire torso from his chest to his back and a samurai's servant with an *Otsu-e* folk art picture of the young maiden of Fuji tattooed on his back. At the final moment, a man quickly rolled up his kimono and said, "Please look here, too." He seized the gaze of everyone present.

"What is this? Isn't your body unmarked? If the color is only white, it's unacceptable. Move aside."

As the organizers attempted to push him away, the man said, "My tattoo is under this and is not one of those cheap designs shown off by the others."

He unwound his new bellyband of white cotton three-and-a-half times to reveal his white abdomen tattooed with a snake having a tongue like a red flame rising above his navel.

"Whaah!"

All ninety-eight people assembled due to pride in their tattoos gasped in admiration. The man was tall and had a fair complexion and favored woodblock print of the tattooed Zhang Shun in the waves. When the surprised faces of those present looked and were convinced even in the twilight light, he wrapped the bellyband around again and, carrying his rolled up kimono under his arm, said, "Pardon me, but I'm a busy man. I will come back to retrieve my rice."

"Oh!"

"Wait!" shouted a voice from behind. A man passed over the handrail of the balcony on the second floor, over the eaves, crawled on his stomach, and grabbed a handhold on the gutter.

"You're under arrest," added Ishihara Risuke, who had been vigilantly watching the group. Before he could jump out onto the balcony and cross over the handrail behind the scoundrel, someone blocked his path and asked, "Excuse me, Captain, please have a look at my tattoo."

"What? Get out of my way."

"Captain Ishihara. Shouldn't you inspect a more interesting tattoo than that tall, skinny snake?"

The person who entangled and pulled back Risuke was a woman of twenty-two or -three years old. She may have been a maid at this venue or a guest at this strange affair.

"Hey, what are you doing? It's your fault a dangerous criminal got away."

Risuke pushed the woman away. During the delay, the mysterious man crossed the same roof, dropped down, and vanished.

Meanwhile, the woman shoved by Risuke got up unperturbed and said, "Is there a problem if a woman has a tattoo?"

An organizer came over and said with a little flattery,

"That is fine. If you join, there will be exactly one hundred participants. Although it's getting chilly, everyone has stripped naked and you must strip too. Do you agree?"

"That's fine. It's no different than going to a public bathhouse."

While speaking, the woman began to undress. With a hint of bashfulness, she revealed her skin.

Two hundred eyes burned with curiosity and cautiously observed from all sides. In the twilight, the hall along the river was bright enough for them to see the mysterious woman expose her beautiful skin.

"Uwaah!"

Admiration rose, not without reason, from one hundred people. A tattoo was inked onto her beautiful, smooth skin like crimson swathed in white habutae silk.

A rat was tattooed on the nape of her neck, a cow and a tiger on her left and right arms, a dragon and a snake on her back, and a rabbit and a horse on her belly.

On her upper torso, seven of the twelve signs of the Chinese zodiac of the rat, the ox, the tiger, the rabbit, the dragon, the snake, and the horse were vividly inked in the two colors of black ink and blood red.

The woman still shy about her body covered her nipples with her palms and rounded her back as if pained by the gazes enveloping her.

At that moment, Ishihara Risuke came flying up the wide staircase like he skipped every other step.

"Where is the woman? She interfered and a criminal escaped."

"I am here, Captain Ishihara."

"Oh!"

Risuke froze. The scent of the semi-nude beautiful woman reached his nose as he panted. Her splendid tattoos were seven of the twelve zodiac signs on her upper torso like indigo pictures drawn on habutae silk.

"Who are you?" he asked.

"Women are a little mischievous," she said.

"What is that tattoo?"

"As you see, they will be the twelve signs of the zodiac. If you wish to see the remaining five, wash your face and come again."

"What do mean, woman?" he asked, as she slipped back into her kimono.

"I will receive the fabric. That is, if all agree…"

When she slightly curved her back like she was about to slip out, Risuke followed close behind her and got in front of her with arms spread.

"Wait, wait. You're probably an accomplice of that rogue who got away. Your body looks like clouds of dust would be released if you were hit. Come with me to the guardhouse."

At that moment,…

"Ah, my wallet's gone."

"My haori coat is gone."

"Oh no, the kimonos are gone."

The crowd panicked. All ninety-eight were naked. The harm was great.

Perhaps, the thieves did their work during the disruption by the man with the snake tattoo and the commotion over the woman's tattoo. Twenty-two or -three attendees were completely nude. The other seventy or so people were not in a position to steal anything.

3

"CAPTAIN, WHAT HAPPENED BACK THERE? Over ninety naked people. Captain, was your plan a mistake?" asked Garappachi. He needled Heiji on the way home after the chaos at Tanemura.

"Ha, ha, is that what you think? I want to say this situation wasn't strange, but the truth is I had a hunch. I imagined that incident was possible."

"Oh?"

"Garappachi, didn't I tell you to keep an eye on your clothes and belongings? You mishear what people say, and it seems you blundered and your wallet was stolen."

"I can't say nothing. The only one who had nothing stolen was you, Captain. You know what's funny. They took Captain Ishihara's tobacco pipe."

"You dope, you talk too much."

"Yeah, it seems so. That pretty woman who tied up Captain Ishihara might have been the thief."

"Do you know that? I didn't go there to find a petty thief. I went to see how many refugees from the Zodiac Twelve Gang would make an appearance."

"The what?"

"You probably know this, too, but at one time the Zodiac Twelve Gang roamed Edo causing trouble. Originally, they came together to punish corrupt samurai who bullied strong men. These twelve comrades were connected to each of the zodiac signs. One of the twelve signs was tattooed on their bodies. Gradually, bad sorts emerged from their group and became extortionists, forgers, night burglars, housebreakers, and even murderers. The twelve ended up disbanding. You must have heard about them," said Heiji with a strange air of confidentiality.

"Well, I heard rumors a couple of years ago," said a sincere Garappachi paying rapt attention.

"Recently, however, strange incidents have occurred."

"Like what?"

"Murders. When I attended the coroner's inquests, each victim had one of the zodiac signs tattooed somewhere on his body."

"What?"

"Well, do you understand the mystery?"

"Nope."

"Your face looked worthy of praise and I thought you understood. Too bad."

"Don't scold me."

While the duo carried on their conversation, they returned to Heiji's house.

Zenigata Heiji never lost his way as much as this time. Recently, there's been a scourge of burglaries, robberies, and housebreaks. These crimes were definitely the work of the Zodiac Twelve Gang who acted boldly over the past few years. The victims thought to be members of the Zodiac Twelve Gang had been stabbed, throttled, and dumped in bodies of water. Because the corpses of five or six men appeared over time, did the Zodiac Twelve Gang split up? A third party and righteous gentleman must be thinking about stealthily killing the Zodiac Twelve.

No possible member of the Zodiac Twelve Gang other than the man with the snake tattoo showed up at The Tattoo Pride Conference. Who was that beautiful woman tattooed with the seven signs of the zodiac on her upper body and tied up by Ishihara Risuke? Heiji wondered with arms folded.

"Captain Zenigata, can you spare a moment?"

The unstained lattice door opened to reveal a follower of Ishihara Risuke, a middle-aged man named Seijiro, in a slight polite bow. He looked much older than Heiji, but favored a merchant more than a police officer and was a highly intelligent man.

The somewhat vacuous Garappachi seemed the perfect partner for the smart Heiji. A mature, traditional detective like Ishihara Risuke needed a follower with worldly wisdom.

"Oh, is that Seijiro? What's the problem?" asked Heiji.

"A terrible thing has occurred. Sergeant Sasano said you must come to Hatchobori."

He dropped the hem of his kimono specked with indigo. His genial face was not the natural personality of a follower of Risuke.

"What has happened?"

"Well, Captain Ishihara brought the woman arrested at Tanemura. When she was examined again, half of her tattoos had disappeared."

"Oh, so that happened?"

"Captain, you knew…"

"I didn't know, but I thought that may happen. In fact, I also used that technique. The six coins on my back were drawn with an ink stick of indigo wax. When moistened, it all wipes off."

"Okay."

"So the captain's tattoo was a fake," said Garappachi.

"Of course. I would hate to sully the body given to me by my parents."

"Okay."

The two followers did not shut their open mouths.

"So why did that woman have a tattoo?" asked Seijiro. Of course, he understood better than Garappachi the vital point of this case.

"If I knew that, this case would be simple. Right now, I only understand a little. As Sergeant Sasano says, 'Don't go when there's no reason to go.' I'd like to collect my thoughts a bit more. I'm sorry, but, Seijiro, would you take Hachi with you to investigate ahead of me?" asked Heiji.

"Yessir."

"As a precaution, wipe the woman's body well, let down her hair, and examine her scalp. If nothing about her scalp is strange, then we have no business with her. If by chance the woman matters, tell Ishihara not to let her go."

"Yessir."

4

THE TWO FOLLOWERS, SEIJIRO and Garappachi, sped to Hatchobori and to the home of Police Sergeant Sasano Shinsaburo. The woman had not been sent to the town magistrate's office yet. A straw woven mat was laid out in the garden and, under candlelight, her body was being wiped down.

"You're a devious woman. These tattoos were drawn on you. What's going on?"

The older-than-forty Ishihara wiping down the skin of the young woman painted an unpleasant picture.

For appearances' sake, the woman's hands were tied behind her back. She twisted her body pitifully under the flickering light as Risuke's rough hands rubbed solid oil on her without the slightest acknowledgment of her.

To their left was the flickering red light, and above was the pale moonlight shining down on her from the right. The two colors distinctly illuminated her face and skin to make her beauty indescribable. The part illuminated by the red light seemed to contort slightly in suffering and charged with traces of heat. The part illuminated by the pale moon seemed to shine a pearl gray and to still all of her passion as serenity.

Sasano Shinsaburo could not bear looking at her and turned his face to gaze at the moon. The eyes of the servants flickered with curiosity from the corners of objects and shadows of buildings as they watched the mysterious scouring of the half-nude woman.

Risuke said, "You shameless woman. Why did you do such a stupid thing? Speak quickly and ask for the mercy of the master."

"..."

"You probably know that man with the snake tattoo. He's suspected of being in the Zodiac Twelve Gang. And you know where he is."

"…"

"It's okay if you don't want to talk. I'm not boasting, but my arms do have a bit of strength. Fortunately, washing off your tattoo gives me the chance to strip your skin. I, Ishihara Risuke, have become a bathhouse attendant. It will be the glory of my life to arrest you."

When Risuke's left hand grabbed hold of the woman's round shoulder, the wet cloth he held in his right hand began to vigorously scour her back starting from her shoulders.

"Ouch!" said the woman while twisting and writhing.

"If you move, my touch gets stronger," said Risuke tightening his grip on her shoulder.

The skin from her shoulders and arms to her back was as beautiful as silk. Risuke's rubbing with ample force caused blood to ooze out before everyone's eyes.

"Mmm."

As she stubbornly pursed her lips, intermittent squeaks resembling blowing into a broken flute accompanied her breaths leaking out.

"Stop Risuke…" said Shinsaburo unable to watch any longer and raised his hand.

Risuke said, "Lord, please let me continue. If I don't, this woman will not easily talk. Damn you, you'll talk. Get the salt," Risuke turned and said to another follower.

At that moment, Garappachi and Seijiro sprinted in.

Garappachi said, "Captain Heiji will come later. Before he gets here, he said to untie the woman's hair and check her scalp. If nothing's there, she's an ordinary woman. If something's there, she's important to this case."

Garappachi took pride in these words that only his captain understood like a prophet.

"All right," answered Risuke with unexpected obedience. He searched for the cord tying her disheveled hair. A follower brought scissors. When he reluctantly cut, her long black hair entangled his hand and pulled backward like water.

"Hey, don't start struggling now, calm down."

Risuke put her head between his knees, pushed aside her disheveled hair, and brought a candle closer.

"Ah!" he flinched. What did he find? The candle tilted and dripped wax onto her cheek.

She didn't complain about being burned, but her enchanting pupils looked up at Risuke's face as if aggrieved by the world.

"What is it, Risuke?"

Without thinking, Shinsaburo stepped down from the porch. When he got close and looked down at her head, in the center of the candlelight he saw the unmistakable tattoo of a rat on her scalp under thick black hair.

"Oh, oh."

She spoke directly to the surprised Shinsaburo, "Don't be so stupid. I'm Boss Osan of the Zodiac Twelve Gang. Breathing your foul breath on me is punishment."

Her impassioned curse hung like a rainbow under the moon.

5

THAT NIGHT WHEN ZENIGATA Heiji raced to Hatchobori, Sasano Shinsaburo's home was in chaos from top to bottom.

Whose hand cut the rope to allow the escape of Osan, the woman boss of the Zodiac Twelve Gang with a rat tattoo on her scalp at the neck and forehead?

"Heiji, you're late. A terrible thing has happened," said Sasano Shinsaburo. The government official had no excuse for not sending her to the magistrate's office and allowing her to escape from his home.

"Lord, now we know that she is Osan of the Zodiac Twelve Gang, the reason becomes clear. There's no need to worry."

Heiji was not surprised and maintained his usual calm. He examined the cut in the rope Osan escaped from.

"You seem to know everything, but please give me a hint."

"Well, I don't know much, but this is certain. Former members of the Zodiac Twelve Gang are alive. There are only three left: Osan with the rat tattoo, Minokichi with the snake tattoo, and Itaro with the boar tattoo. These last three seem to be battling some threat to their lives."

"…"

"We should find Osan's hiding place immediately."

"Where could she have gone?"

"What can be discovered from the pictures of the twelve signs drawn on the woman's skin? By questioning Horitatsu Ago in Ningyocho, who drew the six-coin tattoo on my back, we should find the woman's residence. Goodnight."

Heiji sped from the house in Hatchobori and ran to Ningyocho. The task was simple, just as he thought.

"A young courtesan came. It was right after you went home after the master drew your tattoo. Anyway, Ochaban did it. She ordered only seven of the twelve signs to be drawn beginning above her waist. Since there was no reason to refuse, he carefully drew the design on her in just two hours. I don't know her town. Since she's very beautiful, the young ones were excited after she left. She's not the type of woman seen around here, but they didn't search for her. The master only drew the picture and was delighted. Although she paid us, I think we should've paid her to tattoo one of our designs on her silky skin."

As Horitatsu spoke, he laughed heartily like a master.

Heiji was glib when he left Sasano Shinsaburo to come here, but groaned at the door of Horitatsu before he departed.

6

THIS STORY HAS BEEN a little roundabout, but Osan slipped away from the storeroom after someone cut the rope. She tolerated the slight pain of her body and was led out the back gate. When she went one or two blocks and emerged from a certain alley, another person was there to meet her. The exhausted Osan was slightly suspicious. When she walked in despite herself, she soon came upon a door left ajar. She entered and was pounced on from behind and carried away under a man's arm.

It happened too fast to surprise her. Not only was the untied rope tied up again, this time she was gagged and pulled up to her feet. Given this treatment, it would have been better to have left her tied up, but that probably would have attracted attention.

Osan was carried inside and almost flung down. When she looked all around, a grim-looking young man with a slender face and the obvious shadow of a beard was sitting before her.

"Osan, it's been a while," he said and put on airs as he bit his silver tobacco pipe and smiled a strangely meaningful smile.

"Oh, it's you, Ita…" is what the surprised Osan intended to say, but the gag hindered her speaking. Her eyes reflected the frightening pain she endured and a spark of her indomitable spirit.

"Ha, ha, you remember? What was that between you and me? Osan, there's still some unfinished business. Tonight, I intend to settle that and brought you along. The gag is a bit harsh, but a loud scream would cause problems. Can you put up with it a little while longer? Well? Are you mad? Ha, ha, ha. Perhaps, you don't like the gag. All right, I'll remove it. But if that's a mistake and you scream, I'll take my sword and skewer you like a potato," said Itaro and stood to remove Osan's gag. He wasn't the kind of man to forget he placed his sword in front of the bound Osan.

"Now, this is better. I saved you from that policeman's home in Hatchobori. And that makes me your benefactor, so you should be nice and listen to what I have to say."

No one else was in the area. Everyone except the boss probably went outside. Itaro's green eyes, which only seemed to be deep with spite, stared at the bound breast of Osan as though entangled in her beauty from her face to the nape of her neck.

"Osan, I'll tell you quickly. You and I broke up three years ago. And now the Zodiac Twelve Gang is gone, too, but I could not forget you. When I searched for you, you were living like man and wife with Minokichi, but that appeared to be your evil design. Since that time, Mino went to ruin and became a thief, housebreaker, and killer. In other words, he disgraces the Zodiac Twelve Gang. Fortunately, that awful man had given up and came to see me. Because of recent commercial laws, I've been able to acquire a large sum of money and didn't intend to inconvenience you."

"Shut up!" said Osan unable to hold back.

"What?"

"Shut up and listen. What are you talking about? We broke up because Mino-san robbed and killed. You're talking nonsense. Aren't you a thief and a murderer? Also, I'm scared our old comrades in the Zodiac Twelve will uncover our identities. Didn't you say someone's walking around and killing off each of our comrades one by one? Have you heard who that devil could be? I was the boss of the Zodiac Twelve, and you were Itaro, a beginner, you must stop with this stupid talk."

"You're a loud woman. Can you see me?"

Itaro became more flustered and got close to Osan's breasts.

"Well, please kill me. You are the murdering—"

Before she finished, Itaro gagged her again.

"You're a noisy woman. Speak a little softer. We're not in a secluded house in a field."

"..."

"Think about it for a while. If you're stubborn tomorrow, yours or Minokichi's life will end."

"..."

"I will find where he lives. If I tell Sergeant Sasano, that punk goes to the gallows."

Itaro found the hatred and rage burning in Osan's gorgeous eyes to be amusing and gazed at them for a long time.

107

7

"CAPTAIN, I FOUND HIM."

On the evening of the following day, Garappachi hurtled into Heiji's house like he was tumbling.

"What did you find?" asked Heiji.

"I found that miserable boss. Brace yourself. For one day and one night, I kept on the move without a wink of sleep."

"Garappachi, I was lost in thought and went without sleep, too."

"Well, you can't learn this by thinking. The boss is a guy with a tattoo on the back of his leg."

"Sh! Lower your voice."

"Three of us divided up the work of walking around to each public bathhouse from Hatchobori to Ryogoku. No matter which attendant's booth was asked about a man with a tattoo on the back of his leg. No one had ever seen him."

"So what did you find out?"

"Now here's what you're waiting for. I walked around all day and night and was drenched with sweat. I went to a bathhouse in town. I happened to overhear someone say, 'How about that boss? You can't see what's right in front of your face. He's right here in town. That guy with the tattoo on the back of his leg,'" said Garappachi in a barely audible voice.

"Who is he?"

"Don't be shocked. He's a follower of Captain Ishihara Risuke, that Seijiro—"

"What? What?!"

Heiji was not amazed and ran to Sasano Shinsaburo's residence. After a private talk lasting a minute, he casually summoned Seijiro.

Unaware his evil act had been exposed, Seijiro came without a concern and was seized with great difficulty by Heiji and Garappachi. When he was tied up and the back of his leg examined, near the arch of his foot was a small two-inch tattoo of a boar. They left Seijiro making excuses and rushed to search his home. They instantly grasp the situation. Two or three of his followers were tying Osan up to torture her while she fought back.

ONE MEMBER OF THE ZODIAC Twelve Gang, Itaro, killed each one of his comrades who knew his identity and could get in the way of his own evil acts. He was only cowardly in the face of Osan's beauty, but he made a false step with his last two victims, Minokichi and Osan. While engaged in his deception, Itaro was Seijiro the sensible-looking follower of Risuke, but different in age and appearance, and not a man who would ever be arrested.

They soon discovered Minokichi's hideout. He had been attacked by Itaro and managed to escape the jaws of death. Through the mediation of Heiji, his crime became a minor offense.

While a fugitive, Minokichi went to the Tattoo Pride Conference. Osan guessed his wish to display his incredible snake tattoo. Therefore, she had the tattoo of the twelve zodiac signs drawn on her body to disrupt the conference, and save him from mortal danger.

Heiji struggled for a long time because he could not decipher the secrets of the Zodiac Twelve Gang. He deduced the rat on Osan's scalp and the snake wrapped around Minokichi's torso and concluded Itaro's boar must be on the back of his leg. He realized the tattoos of the Zodiac Twelve Gang were in places unseen by the world.

The aim of this tale was to tell the story of this romance on the first page of the development of tattoos. Minokichi and Osan became a happy couple with the sympathy of Heiji. There was no intent here to write about the longevity of an honest life.

CHAPTER EIGHT

THE WOMAN IN LOVE WITH BELLS

1

"HACHI, FOLLOW THAT ONE."

"Okay."

"Don't let 'em get away, your opponent is the slender one."

"That worn-out ronin?"

"Idiot! He's a samurai like Buddha and is a calligraphy teacher somewhere. I'm talking about the young woman walking ahead of him."

"Okay, that pretty, young wife is a ruffian? That's a surprise."

"Lower your voice or people will hear."

Zenigata Heiji and his sidekick Garappachi were on their way to visit Tokuzo Inari, the god of fertility and fortune, at the prosperous Shitaya Shrine. While still morning, they passed before Koutoku-ji Temple on their way to Ueno.

"Garappachi, look carefully and speak to gain knowledge."

"Okay."

Heiji spoke in a quieter tone.

"The samurai is a little scary looking, but look closely at him. His deeply etched face does not look malicious. The reasoning is identical to no horns for a beast with fangs and no fangs for a beast with horns. A man with that scary-looking face is most likely a pleasant fellow. However, a truly evil or wicked man would have an unbelievably smooth face. If you look closely, you can see it from here. That red staining the end of that samurai's sleeve proves he's a calligraphy master. The front edge of his sleeve touches the vermilion inkstone when he corrects a child's handwriting."

"Okay, so what's the proof that pretty, young woman is evil?"

"When we brushed past her, similarly, the end of her sleeve was stained red, but hers was not vermilion but red blood. And that young woman seems to have been dispossessed of the fox spirit clay figure from her sleeve in front of the Koutoku-ji Temple."

"I saw that, too. They sell figures in front of the gate at Tokuzo Inari. An unglazed clay fox is painted with watercolors. One costs twelve mon. They say if you hide it in your pocket, your wish comes true. Some gamblers carry them around."

"That fox hidden in the sleeve of the young woman seems cute, but when she happened to drop it, the tail snapped off on the dry road. Look here."

When had Heiji picked it up? He pulled out and showed the clay fox figurine with the broken tail.

"When did you pick that up, Captain? You work fast."

"Keep your voice down, dummy. Are the passers-by looking at us? When a woman drops something, no matter how much of a hurry I'm in, I usually stop to pick it up for her. It's useless, but if it's damaged, my regret is I try to restore it to its original state even if it's a trifling object. But what about that young woman?"

"When she dropped the fox and its tail broke off, she didn't look back or try to pick it up but hurried away. Of course, that's odd."

"You understand, Hachi? That woman is either stupid or extraordinary. If not, she does not worry easily, and that is very unusual. It was not easy for her to throw away and abandon the magical fox for granting her wish."

Heiji's insight invigorated Garappachi.

"Hey, Captain. Would you leave this job to me?"

"Why?"

"As the first distinguished exploit of Hachigoro, I will expose everything."

"Are you sure, Garappachi?"

"Am I sure? You make me a little sad."

"..."

"First, it would be no good if word gets out that Captain Zenigata Heiji and his man Hachigoro are after that young wife, who may fly away."

"That's true. If you don't make any mistakes, you won't lose sight of her. I will go back to Tokuzo Inari and wait there for you."

"Thanks. Leave it to me, Captain."

"Don't mess up. Your rival is the pretty, young wife."

"I'll be okay."

Garappachi's passed the palm of his hand over his forehead and left Heiji to trail the woman.

2

AS EXPECTED, HEIJI WENT to Tokuzo Inari and walked into an unbelievable major incident.

Deities go in and out of fashion, and today, no traces remain of some. However, that day an incident occurred. A crowd gathering since the morning was packed before the gate of the very popular Tokuzo Inari. Heiji quickened his pace and cut through the crowd. When he emerged, someone said, "Ah! Captain Zenigata. Perfect timing."

The speaker appeared to be an eloquent townsman Heiji recognized who pulled Heiji's sleeve to lead him.

"What happened? What is this?" Heiji asked.

"It was a terrible mistake. Please look there."

He pointed under the small decorative fence surrounding the shrine.

"Eeyah, this is awful," said Heiji.

Although Heiji said he hated dead bodies and brutal scenes, he often went to see them but had never seen anything this peculiar.

A middle-aged man tied up with a new red and white bell cord had been stabbed two or three times with a dagger and suffered a cruel death.

"Here he is, Captain Zenigata. He was the temple keeper Jinzaburo and a popular man around town. He's not the sort to be resented. He didn't care about hoarding money. This outrageous situation was discovered early this morning by a visitor. Please hunt down this criminal."

"Someone committed this horrible act. The temple keeper was killed in front of the fence. Is this the story of a curse?" Heiji asked while examining the corpse from head to toe. He was a sturdy man of forty-five or -six years old and had no links to any women or children. Although morning was mentioned, the incident occurred during the day. Perhaps, he was knocked out by a blow, and then tied up with the bell cord, but later came to and could speak, so he was stabbed wildly with a dagger.

At a time when pedestrian traffic was light, the corpse lay beside the fence. Even for an hour or a half hour after dawn, people passed by without noticing the body. Eventually, a visitor to the temple noticed the cord wrenched off the bell hanging in the front shrine and rushed out in panic. Soon the bound body of the temple keeper was discovered beside the fence seen by few people.

Before the inspection by government officials, Heiji quickly looked all around. Other than the large bell hanging above the offering box and the red and white bell cord attached to the bell, nothing else was out of place. At any time, somewhere in the world, there are people called Offering Box Scum. The skilled ones fish out coins with birdlime. The sloppy ones break open the box. Apparently, there are quite a few of them.

"Let me see."

A man like Zenigata Heiji had folded his arms and was at a loss for what to do.

Curious onlookers flocked to the front of Tokuzo Inari.

"Jinzaburo's been killed."

"What kind of punk would kill a nice guy like him?"

"And the fence has been defiled by the blood. That beast is probably cursed. The deity Oinari-sama won't stay silent."

Heiji heard snippets of rumors. There was something deeper in this incident. Finally, he paid a visit to the souvenir shop in front of the gate. The morning pilgrims took no notice of the shop. Unfortunately, it had just opened, and the shop worker knew nothing.

"Did a pretty, young woman around eighteen or nineteen years old buy a fox charm?"

"Yeah, one probably did. I sell twenty or thirty foxes every day, but I don't remember anyone in particular. In a place like this, geisha and teahouse ladies buy them a lot."

The memory of the proprietress of the souvenir shop was no help at all.

3

"WAIT A MINUTE, MISTER," said the young woman and stopped. She was eighteen or nineteen years old but did not appear to live in a mansion or a tradesman's home. Her clever-looking oval face had traces of being a tease, but she was probably well raised and somehow dignified as well as being fairly pretty and cute.

"..."

Her attack was sudden, and Garappachi crouched in the middle of the street. Although deep in autumn, he wore a gloomy striped cotton cloth tucked in to cover his head from the morning sun. He looked like a balancing toy with his clenched left fist, which looked unfavorable in any light.

"This is my home. You've been following me. Now, go home."

"Okay."

"You're a dopey wolf."

"Ah!"

Her confident, sharp words rained down on his blank face, then she disappeared down an alley. For a short time, Garappachi forgot all about following her and stood like he was mulling over her words.

"Oh, no!"

He let her flee into the alley. In this winding shortcut of an alley, the young woman evaporated like a rainbow.

"Dammit!"

He snapped his tongue. He failed at the big job he had been waiting to get for a long time and felt only shame. When he returned to the main street he left that morning, he happened to pass by the residence of the samurai from earlier. It was the residence of the ronin in his fifties Heiji decided was a calligraphy teacher.

"I'll hang around this samurai's house so I won't feel guilty about following the young woman," he said while waiting a short time until the worn-out, faded ronin passed by and then began to trail him. They soon arrived at the main street and turned a few times down an alley, somewhere in the alley Garappachi thought, This time, you're not getting away.

He tailed close behind the ronin, like he was about to step on his heels, and always kept him in sight.

"Hey, townsman."

"Yes, yes."

"You've been following me for some time. What is your business?"

"What? You're mistaken."

"If you're a robber or a thief, give up and go home. A ronin like me with no stipend isn't carrying around even one mon. Also, I may be old, but I have skills," said the ronin as he laughed aloud. The relaxing of the lines on his deeply etched face and the traces of navy beard stubble made him charming.

"Um, I'm not a bad guy," said Garappachi.

"That may be so. Even if I read too much into your face, it's not the face of a bad man. Your nose is turned up, the corners of your eyes droop, and your teeth have a few gaps. Your pockmarked face points to a good man or a dunce."

"Oh, my."

"A bad man would have a more expressionless face and be grim."

Garappachi was dumbfounded.

"The captain says stuff like that too. That samurai's face is a little grim, but he's definitely a Buddha."

"Not quite a Buddha, well, that's all right. Please tell me, why were you following me?"

"I wasn't following you, master. I was wondering about where that pretty, young woman, who went out a little before you, has gone to, so..."

"You idiot."

"Okay."

"Because of fools like you, young women can't walk around alone. Only today, I will overlook this, now go home."

"Okay."

Garappachi was vanquished. He hurried past a few blocks as the ronin waited for him to disappear into an alley. When Garappachi asked at a neighborhood sake shop, he found out the ronin was from Kyushu and called Shirakawa Tetsunosuke. They said he wasn't rich, and his life was untroubled. He didn't seek other government services but wandered aimlessly every day.

"That ronin's got a bunch of calligraphy students together to teach them," said Garappachi.

"No, I never heard that story. He's alone with no family or friends. Other than going out from time to time, he only reads books filled with gibberish."

"That's it!" said Garappachi when he heard that and jumped up to run to Tokuzo Inari. Losing sight of the woman was definitely a major blunder, but judging that ronin to be a calligraphy teacher was Captain Heiji's mistake. He thought the odds may be five-to-five or seven-to-three, but the captain's scolding should be softened.

When he arrived at the front of Tokuzo Inari, the crowd was thick.

"'Scuse. Beg your pardon," Garappachi said as he made his way through the curious onlookers. There in front of the temple keeper's corpse bound with the red and white bell cord under the fence was Zenigata Heiji with arms folded.

"Captain, what happened?"

"Oh, Hachi. What happened to the woman?"

"I trailed her to Iriya but lost her when she slipped into a secret passage of a scary maze."

"What? You lost her? You dope."

"But Captain, I am sure that ronin is not a calligraphy teacher."

"Who wanted to know that? A dunce. Go over there."

"Okay."

Garappachi was shattered.

4

THE MURDER OF THE TEMPLE keeper at Tokuzo Inari was judged to be nothing more than the work of a common criminal. Zenigata Heiji conducted various searches but found nothing.

Jinzaburo was isolated and had no money, no dependents, and no grudges held against him. The offering box was undamaged. The only item taken was the bell in the front shrine. When the bell cord was yanked off to tie up Jinzaburo, the parts that tumbled down may have been picked up by someone and taken away.

However, the deeply superstitious and curious onlookers of the day could not accept that the bell in the front shrine of Inari-sama was hidden somewhere.

Was the bell stolen for a reason?

These thoughts popped into Heiji's mind. But a bell in the worship hall of a shrine was not an object that is stolen; this conflicted with superstitions. First, the small shrine was foreclosed, and a rich man recently made a donation to plan for starting renovations. Naturally, the old bells would be replaced with new ones. If the proper procedures were followed, the bells could probably have been obtained cheaply. No matter how he thought about it, that sort of theft would not lead to murder.

Nevertheless, what kind of clue was that young woman's escape? Only this time, Heiji, who was thinking about his follower, didn't speak to Garappachi for half the day. It was a failure to lose sight of the woman with blood clinging to the ends of her sleeve because of a small mistake after she left the grounds.

The final step was to investigate the whereabouts of the bell. Within the day, Heiji rounded up his men to ask around neighborhood secondhand shops and shrines.

"The captain's judgment is not cloudy but is on target."

The first to run in was Garappachi.

"What happened?" asked Heiji and jumped up.

"I heard from secondhand shops in Shitaya that lately, people have been buying up bells," said Garappachi.

"Is that true, Hachi?"

"Is it true? You're cruel. I walked on these legs and heard with these ears. There's no mistake. And bells have been stolen a few times from the worship halls of temples and shrines."

"What?"

"Captain, where are the bells being collected. There are definitely plotters, maybe it's a rebellion."

"You are a fool. Are the bells going to be changed into bullets? Were men or women walking around buying those bells?"

"Both men and women and samurai and townsmen."

"Around when did this begin?"

"Incidents cropped up over the last six months. The violent one was a few days ago."

"All right, I understand. Hachi."

"Yes."

"You've said that you'd give your life to save mine at any time," said a more serious Heiji.

"Yes, I did. While fearful, Koban Gold Hachigoro would not spare his money or his life."

"Even if you don't spare your money, you don't have any."

"That's right. The captain's sharp eye is not clouded."

"Fortunately, you only have one life, so will you loan that?"

"That's an easy favor. Should I do my best, or will I be used as normal?"

"You are a dope."

In this vein, an Edokko of old would stake his life without a thought after making that pronouncement.

"Don't tell anyone. Our colleagues are gathering as many bells as possible. I also told Kuma and Sanko. They're gathering bells from the unreachable outskirts, loading them on their backs, and you will soon walk around selling these bells."

"That's not so bad. I'll do it."

"The fellows searched for bells with bloodshot eyes and had no technique other than to fish for bells."

"I understand, Captain. I'll walk around selling temple bells or fire bells," said the plain-thinking Garappachi and rushed out with every intention of succeeding.

5

THE NEXT DAY, HACHIGORO became a bell vendor and walked from Iriya to Negishi. He wore protectors covering the backs of his hands and leggings, an unfashionable lined kimono, and a worn-out hand towel. No one would know what he was by looking at him, but he carried a peddler's placard. A box of small bells hung from the shoulders of the bell peddler. In each hand, he carried a mix of five or six large bells, old and new.

"Bells, bells. Anyone need a bell? The big ones are bells from worship halls. The small ones are scissors bells. The bells hanging from my waist are both new and old. I have gold bells, silver bells, brass bells, copper bells, knee bells, hand bells, bracelet bells, bells for long swords, and bells from burial grounds. And there are bells for dogs, bells for hawks, and anything called a bell. Anyone need a bell?"

As he shouted this, from time to time, Garappachi peeked at a sleeve and misread the message written in kana characters. In that era of walking around and catching fleas from cats, selling bells was not remarkable.

"Excuse me, bell seller."

Once in a while, Hachigoro was called over to sell bells for kittens and bells for scissors, but no one was interested in the large bells like the one stolen from Tokuzo Inari.

The following day, Garappachi went to the interior of Negishi. Now comfortable, he smoothly delivered his message without peeking at his sleeve. Because the bells weren't being sold for money, his carefree notion was that he could quit, but not because selling bells was bad.

"Bells for sale. Do you need a bell? Hand bells, knee bells, bracelet bells!" he shouted.

"Wait a minute, bell seller."

The wicket gate in the black fence behind a dormitory of a mansion opened, and a young woman waved him over.

"Yes. Yes."

"The young missus wishes to see the bells. Please come this way."

"Yes. Yes."

With this invitation, he hurried into the garden. The wicket gate shut tight behind him. When he took the opportunity to turn and look, the woman who called him was the young woman wearing the kimono with the bloodstained sleeve three or four days earlier. He had trailed her from the front of Koutoku-ji Temple, but she gave him the slip in Iriya.

"Ah!" yelped Garappachi without thinking, but acted like he stumbled over a garden rock. The situation completely changed. His head towel was wrapped in the Yoshiwara style, and he thought she might not recognize him. He was the ever-optimistic Garappachi as he followed the woman around the garden of the dormitory.

"Miss, the bell seller is here," the maid called through the shoji screen door.

"Very good, Yae," she kindly responded and edged up to and opened the screen door on the autumn morning. She looked to be twenty-two or - three years old and sickly but was a gorgeous woman. Without thinking, Garappachi snatched off his head wrap and bowed.

The deep-blue traces of her slender eyebrows were strangely desolate. The toenails of her bare feet resembling seashells, a beautiful style of the

Genroku era, were lined up on the door threshold. A pearl-colored haze hung down from her hips. Coming from above the mist, Garappachi heard an elegant voice and surrendered.

"You came from downtown, it's rare for a bell seller to come to this area. What kind of goods do you have? Please, show me every last one. If I'm intrigued, I will buy a few."

"Yes. Okay."

Finally, the dumbstruck Garappachi came to his senses and hurried to open his box of bells.

However, at that time, in the shadows of the lantern, behind the doors, and in the corners of the veranda, the eyes of several people shined like savage beasts trained on food. Hachigoro was a little concerned.

When he arranged all the bells in the box and held them in his hands, the pretty maid who escorted Hachigoro raised her hand to signal.

"Now!"

From all sides, women rushed in. All manner of maids, chambermaids, seamstresses, and cooks ran out and surrounded Hachigoro.

"Eehyaah! What are you doing?" he said as they closed in on him. Although he thought women treated people with kindness, without a word, they covered him with a wrapping cloth, bound him with obi sashes, and hauled him inside.

6

AFTER THREE DAYS, GARAPPACHI had not returned home. Zenigata Heiji took action.

When he visited Sergeant Sasano Shinsaburo, Ishihara Risuke was talking about a yakuza named Senkichi, who lived next to Tokuzo Inari, as the murderer of the temple keeper. He was a gambler with money troubles and targeted Jinzaburo's wallet.

If Jinzaburo had a secret stash, it was not properly locked up. In fact, the thief carefully concocted this evil plan to sneak into Jinzaburo's room to steal his horde. He climbed onto the offering box to tear the cord off the bell and finally carried the body out to the fence.

"That is not so. The murderer is probably an unbelievably important man," said Heiji and left the sergeant's home. Although he spoke with confidence, he didn't have one lead to trace.

For safety's sake, Heiji returned to Shitaya to talk to a parishioner Soudai, the owner of a drinking establishment in town called Izumiya, and was given an incredible new fact.

He was told that the buildings at Tokuzo Inari were ancient, and a donation had been given for entirely new buildings, which included arranging to provide wood by next spring when construction was set to begin. The donor was Okawaya Magosaburo, an elite grain wholesaler in Horidome with money and businesses in various domains. He also had permission to bear a surname and wear a sword.

It would have been fine if it were only that, but the faithful Magosaburo accepted moving the old temple and all its fittings except for the main Buddha image to the expansive garden of the Negishi dormitory to be enshrined.

"All the parishioners will be overjoyed to have everything from the offering box to the bell rope replaced with new ones. Nevertheless, they said it would be a shame to hand everything over to Okawaya-san in an untidy state. That's why the decorative fence and the shrine archway were painted. Only the wooden magnolia latticework was painted red. We had no idea the trouble this would cause. Through the efforts of the captain, all of the parishioners would like to see this murderer captured as soon as possible."

After hearing the story about the proprietor of Izumiya, the dark chest of Heiji was illuminated.

"Thank you. I have a better understanding now. Because they say there is punishment by Inari-sama, the murderer probably knows this, too. Thank you for your time."

Heiji rushed out of Izumiya with the target of Okawaya in Negishi. Of course, he couldn't imitate Garappachi and go out as a bell seller. As a detective, in his dependable work clothes, he walked around beyond the wooden fence about four blocks in all directions.

Heiji asked around the neighborhood and found that the master Okawaya was a forty-year-old man in his prime who lost his wife young. He bought out of prostitution a courtesan in Yoshiwara he knew well for a few years. With the consent of relatives, he made her his second wife. She was a mysterious and prudent woman as well as beautiful and loving. She was sickly and not taken to his home in Horidome. He spared no expense to build a fine dormitory in Negishi as her home.

That woman was called Kome and, for some reason, loved the sounds of bells. The house was filled with the many bells she bought over a long time. When he heard a bell to call a servant or to call for a meal, Heiji became ecstatic.

He entered the gate and listened carefully and could hear the charming sounds of bells coming from somewhere and echoing in the autumn air.

"This is the place," said Heiji to himself and walked through the entryway.

A LARGE BELL DANGLED in the entrance of the dormitory. Around that time, while thinking of this as the mansion of bells, two or three clangs rang out. In this rare approach, he smoothly slid open the door of the entrance.

"Who is it?" tentatively asked the unforgettable young woman, who had been tailed by Garappachi. This saucy young woman spoke with cutting words.

"Ah, of course, you live here."

"..."

The young woman blushed and seemed about to shut the shoji screen when Heiji said, "Wait a moment. My name is Heiji, and I'm here on government business. You are suspected of murdering Jinzaburo at Tokuzo Inari. Any attempts to mislead will not benefit you. Be quiet and get your husband. Now, if you don't tell me why you collected the bells, I cannot understand what this is about."

Heiji behaved professionally and kindly to make sure she understood. The young woman looked down but seemed determined.

She said, "Please wait a moment," and quietly disappeared inside.

He waited for a short time and then passed through into an inner parlor that wasn't big but was neat and tidy.

"Excuse me for making you wait. You are Captain Zenigata? It is wonderful to meet you. I am Kome, the wife of Okawaya."

She quietly greeted him from beside the door threshold and no longer looked like a beautiful geisha, but behaved like a sophisticated, attractive wife.

"Please understand your troublesome strategy was a mistake. I had a man, Garappachi, disguise himself as a bell peddler. What happened to him?"

Heiji's tone was subdued but unyielding.

She said, "Yes, yes, he didn't identify himself, and I imagined he was spying for my enemy. He was loitering near this dormitory for a while."

"So it seems. It's terrible to hear he was exposed, but I would like to hear your story. Next, I want to hear about the bell at Tokuzo Inari. What happened there?" said Heiji whose words went straight to the heart of the problem.

She said, "I know a little about that. Earlier, my young maid Yae went out on my behalf to visit the shrine to keep an eye on that bell day and night. However, when she went to look on that day, she said the red and white cord of the bell had been torn off and a dead body bound by the bell cord was under the decorative fence. Because Yae is a strong girl, she searched near the body thinking the bell may be there, but there was no bell. At that time, the edge of her sleeve was sullied by a small blood smear."

Kome's answer was clear. The beautiful mistress with blue traces of eyebrows was reminiscent of former prosperity and had an intelligence not matching her age or character.

"That seems to be true. She had no reason to cut the bell cord. Although strong-willed, she had no reason to kill Jinzaburo. Recently, she passed by me on the street, and I was surprised by the sight of blood on her sleeve. I saw Jinzaburo's body and knew this was not the work of a woman or a child. Thank you for clearing that up," said Heiji politely in words and attitude, in contrast to an ordinary detective. At first, Kome spoke with caution but gradually came to trust Heiji.

She asked, "Is there anything else you would like to know?"

"Please tell me a few more things. Why are you collecting so many bells? What do you intend to do with them? And you mistook Hachigoro for your enemy's spy. Who is this enemy? If you tell me, my business here will end."

"Yes, I cannot keep this a secret and will tell you everything. If my father were alive, I would never say a word, no matter what, but now, that story is old," said Kome in her elegant way of speaking.

8

KOME'S FATHER WAS A CHRISTIAN samurai named Yoshimura Michinojo and a remnant of those defeated at Shimabara. Before a riot sparked the Shimabara Rebellion, seven comrades traveled incognito to Edo to instigate an incident in the territory of the shogun. However, the rebellion was swiftly put down, and the foundation of the Tokugawa shogunate was unshakable. When the pauper ronin understood they had no options, the seven comrades agreed to scatter. As the central figure of this group, Yoshimura Michinojo was connected to his conspirators for a long time.

Later, his plan was to adopt a Dutch-style metal jewelry taught by Amakusa and create elaborate bells. He took the name of Yoshimura Dousai and gained popularity among collectors in Edo, but he wasn't expert and didn't become rich. To all appearances, he was a poor, middle-aged man with a wife and a daughter.

After his wife Oya died, his only keepsakes were her unique golden hairpins, which he cast to create a large bell that was hung in his workroom. Day and night, he enjoyed its clear sound. But one evening, a night burglar broke in, stabbed Yoshimura Dousai, and stole every bell.

Dousai lived until the following day. Until he succumbed to his fatal wounds, he kept repeating, "My enemy is Kawai Ryunosuke. My enemy is Kawai Ryunosuke."

Kawai Ryunosuke was a ronin from the western part of Japan and always friendly with her father Dousai. Perhaps, he knew her father worked as the liaison of the seven remnants from Shimabara and possessed a book of names and locations, and tried to steal it. If the names and locations of the seven from Shimabara were known, blackmailing or informing on them would be worth a fortune.

Kome, his only daughter, became a prostitute in Yoshiwara to find clues about the villain. With her natural beauty and intelligence, for a time, she was reputed to be at the height of her powers and bought out of prostitution by Okawaya Magosaburo. Although her present life was comfortable, her body was at ease, but her spirit was troubled. She was unable to forget the beautiful sound of the bell created long ago by her father Dousai.

With the permission of her husband Magosaburo, she spared no expense to buy all types of old and new bells and searched for one inscribed with Dousai. Strangely, she never found her father's final masterpiece cast from her mother's golden hairpins.

As her investigation progressed, that bell had been sold by someone and discovered in the front shrine in Tokuzo Inari. This bell was the one she desired. She may have felt uneasy like it was a trick of the deity Inari-sama. Instead of donating the entire main shrine building, all the old shrines were received and moved to the dormitory in Negishi. She intended to become familiar day and night with the clear sounds of the inscribed bell — the final work of her father that hung in the front shrine.

"Those are the reasons. Captain, please understand my feelings of yearning for the sounds of the bell made by my father."

Kome finished the long story and looked up plaintively at Heiji.

9

"CAPTAIN, WHAT'S GONNA HAPPEN now?" asked Garappachi.

Heiji said, "I don't know. Since you were detained in a dormitory resembling an island of women, even if it was only two days, you must have become a little wiser. What do you think will happen?"

"Well, my hands and feet were tied up, and I was tossed in a storeroom. There's no such thing as that scary island of women, but that night-soil cook still scares me stiff."

"Don't gripe Hachi."

Zenigata Heiji and Hachigoro carried on this conversation as they left the dormitory in Negishi.

When they reached Iriya, Heiji was overwhelmed by a thought and stopped in the road.

"Hachi, you said that ronin was not a calligraphy teacher."

"What?"

"During the morning of the incident, that samurai we encountered in front of Koutoku-ji Temple. The one you trailed."

"Heh, heh, the storytellers say even the prudent man slips up. Only that one time, the captain's insight was clouded."

"Enough of your silly talk. If that samurai is not a calligraphy teacher, the red on his sleeve was not vermilion ink but red paint."

"What?"

"The proprietor of Izumiya said the wooden magnolia latticework had just been painted red. To rip out that bell in the front shrine, the thief had to climb onto the offering box. If his footing was bad and he was unsteady when he took the bell, wouldn't his sleeve rub against the painted latticework?

"Aahah, I see."

"And Okawaya's courtesan said Kawai Ryunosuke killed her father. If alive, he would be a man over fifty and have a grim face with dreadful whiskers."

"What?"

"Come on, Garappachi. You will have an unexpected success from failure. Take me to that ronin's house."

"This way Captain."

10

THE DUO NEARLY FLEW THROUGH the air to the row house of the ronin Shirakawa Tetsunosuke. When they peeked through the lattice, they saw a house filled with bells. The owner Tetsunosuke was peacefully napping in the rays of the autumn sun leaking through the shoji-papered door.

"Hello. Hello. Excuse me," said Hachigoro and slid open the door. Next, he said, "Shirakawa Tetsunosuke, you're under arrest!"

Zenigata Heiji rushed inside with him. As expected, the ronin drew his long sword and asked, "What's going on?!"

Heiji dashed straight toward him and used his signature throw to flick coins at him. One smack made his fist release the sword. Another smacked Tetsunosuke hard between his eyebrows.

"Ow!"

Tetsunosuke winced, fell back and doubled over, and then was tightly bound in an instant. Fitting his personality, Garappachi's strength was enormous and, at times like this, was unexpectedly useful.

NOT LONG AFTER, Kawai Ryunosuke's head was displayed at the execution grounds in Suzugamori.

He went around stealing bells from temples and shrines because he realized the names and locations of the remaining rebels at Shimabara were written inside the bell he stole when he killed Dousai and later sold. He did not bring the case to a court of law and had no associations with higher-level government officials. Among the bells seized from Kawai's home, not one had the names and locations written inside.

Understandably, only the bell stolen from Tokuzo Inari was returned to Kome's hands from the hands of Zenigata Heiji. When that bell was split in two, something was written in a very tiny script. Of course, Heiji never read it.

At some later date, Heiji paid a visit to Sergeant Sasano Shinsaburo, as if nothing had happened, Heiji said, "By now, the remaining Shimabara rebels would be two or three decrepit old men and living in Edo. They were searched for and would have been useful. I heard something more important. The exploit of arresting Kawai Tetsunosuke was not my success, but Garappachi's. That man is not so stupid after all. Please take this occasion to praise him."

CHAPTER NINE

THE STONE DEITY WITH HUMAN SKIN

1

IN THE AGE OF KANEYASU during the Edo era, a few miles outside of Sugamo and Otsuka was countryside covered with fields of rice and other crops, and trees and bushes as in Musashino.

Before reaching Koshinzuka and outside the imposing earthen walls of the residence of the wealthy Kuroki Magoemon grew a cluster of five or six trees. Among the trees was a stone statue of Jizo, the guardian deity of travelers and children. Although its nose and ears were broken off, its merciful eyes drooped and enshrined Buddha in a joyous appearance.

Shops and houses stood beside Itabashi Road, and it could justifiably be described as desolate. Merchants and villagers going in and out of the estate of Kuroki Magoemon had to pass by this Jizo. The age and identity of this image of Buddha out in the open were unknown. Its circumstances were pitiful because the people who occasionally provided meals to the priest never provided a bib to the Jizo.

Who knows when it began, but the skin of the Jizo that should have been cold was discovered to be lukewarm like that of a human. Perhaps, children from the village were the first to notice while playing a game of tag nearby. Soon adults found out and it became a sensation in Sugamo, Otsuka, and Komagome.

"The skin of Jizo-sama is warm! That's ridiculous! This Jizo is chiseled from stone and his nose is missing. The sun probably warmed it up."

People who dismissed the rumor spoke like that, while others paid absolutely no attention to them.

"Don't be so flip. If you think it's a lie, go and touch it. In the morning before the sun's rays hit, it is warm, and when the sun is high, it slowly gets colder. They say that's because this Jizo goes to bed at night just like us. Is it divine punishment?"

The superstitious people of the day had no response.

The strange miracle was that the stone Jizo in the field was rumored to be warm like human skin. That was the rumor, but no one tried to see whether it was true. The rumor said that if a perforated brass coin was placed on the stone pedestal of the Jizo, then the following morning you would find it had changed into a gold coin.

People today may have difficulty believing that a brass coin on the stone pedestal of the Jizo would transform into a gold coin overnight, but the naive and carefree people of those days accepted miracles.

"I'm telling you, put a brass coin or the most worthless coin you have on that Jizo, and it will turn into a shiny gold or silver coin."

"I'll try it. Lend me a little capital."

"What are you saying? If I'm gonna lend you money, I might as well take it there myself. That sort of easy moneymaking is pretty rare."

This exchange often occurred. In fact, a brass or a near worthless coin placed on the stone pedestal of the Jizo with human skin sometimes changed into an oval or a circular silver coin, but rarely into a gold coin.

The transformation was astounding. A coin on the stone pedestal did not necessarily change every night, but strangely incited a perilous superstition. Before ten days passed, the Jizo with human skin of Sugamo gained popularity and respect as a god of fortune.

The real name of the sidekick of the famous lawman Zenigata Heiji, was Hachigoro, also known as Garappachi, who was also a popular man. On the way home after going to the region of Koshinzuka on his captain's business, he soon discovered a crowd in a field and indulged himself by snooping around. He found proof in less than an hour. When he returned to Kanda and told the story with much gesturing, Heiji was not as interested as usual in Garappachi's story and impatiently said, "Hmmm. That technique is new. Before ten days pass, a transformation is certain. Fortunately, I'm putting government business in order, so you should observe that place for a while."

"I should? Do I have to go to Sugamo every day?"

"Don't speak such nonsense. If you examine the details of the scheme, our rival will be a challenge. If you watch carefully, it won't look absurd."

"Really?"

Although he had no clue why, Garappachi haunted Sugamo from that day on.

2

"CAPTAIN, THIS IS BAD!"

"What, Garappachi? Is it your usual anxiety? Don't get so upset. Calm down and tell me quietly."

"I can't say it quietly. I just ran all the way from Sugamo."

"What happened? Did Jizo-sama start dancing?"

"I wouldn't be surprised if that happened. Somehow the miraculous Buddha was warm like human skin every morning."

"You're oddly calm. Something is very strange?"

Zenigata Heiji's interest was piqued slightly.

"Magoemon, the wealthy head of the Kuroki family, and the peasants of the land were in a standoff. Even now, blood is raining down in unrest."

"That is serious. What's the reason for the standoff?"

"It's the gift. The miraculous Jizo-sama that changes brass and nearly worthless coins into silver and gold coins. The greedy Kuroki said it made sense to move Jizo-sama onto his estate because it's in his field."

"Of course."

"But the local people don't agree. Without a doubt, the field belongs to Kuroki, but Jizo-sama has been at the same place for a very long time. No one knows who created it or put it up. Even the power of a rich man is not that of a god or Buddha-sama."

"That's interesting."

"There's something even more interesting. A peasant uprising. Twenty or thirty of Kuroki's employees showed up with wooden swords and short spears. When they tried to move Jizo-sama inside the estate, the local people armed with hoes, sickles, and bamboo armor appeared to keep that from happening. Sugama was a full-scale battlefield. Captain, you have to go and do something. If this is ignored, people are sure to be hurt."

Garappachi was earnest, but Heiji was not surprised at all.

"Forget it. Leave it alone. Look past that storm in a teacup. To be sure, some ass is vomiting his red tongue somewhere. Perhaps, that disturbance is some sort of stage direction. Without further information on this matter, our job is not to interfere."

Heiji spoke his mind while his fingertips turned his pipe round and round.

As he predicted, after Garappachi rushed to make his report, Kuroki came to a compromise with the local people.

They settled on moving the stone Jizo-sama inside the Kuroki estate, but the local people could freely come and go, and were allowed to pray or make money or votive offerings as always.

The location of the stone Jizo was a place with aged granite weighing at most around twelve or thirteen *kanme* and a product of hard times. Carrying the Jizo just sixty yards from the middle of the brush into the Kuroki estate may not have mattered from the beginning.

What was meant by inside the estate was the back door of the north storehouse. A six-foot-wide path extended into the residence and was fenced in on both sides. Few changes were made outside the estate.

Jizo-sama was moved there and immediately adorned with a bib. Incense and flowers were offered. It became unrecognizably luxurious within the day. Eventually, a roof to shelter from the rain was built. Needless to say, Kuroki contributed, summoned a carpenter from Edo, and proceeded with the plan the day after estimates were finished.

3

SADLY, KUROKI STILL HAD not touched the skin of the Jizo, skin with the softness and warmth of a virgin's skin. Magoemon usually scowled because he thought it made him look dignified. He could not act foolishly by touching the Jizo's skin in front of the local peasants and villagers.

The following morning, Kuroki jumped out of bed at daybreak. Before he saw anyone in the area, he examined the stone pedestal of Jizo-sama and tried to touch Jizo-sama's skin during the morning when it was said to be warm like human skin.

The sight of the fifty-year-old Kuroki tiptoeing to sneak up to Jizo-sama was bizarre. Fortunately, no one was in the area to bear witness.

He stayed close to the fence as he walked around under the faint morning light. Kuroki thought he hallucinated a Jizo as precious as all money. The Jizo with human skin that should have been on the stone pedestal was toppled onto the damp ground. Also, the area was trampled with the impressions of human footsteps.

"What is this?"

Kuroki's hand rested on Jizo's shoulder. Was his hand trembling under the touch of skin far from being like human skin but more like ice?

That wasn't the only strange element. He was surprised by the state of Jizo-sama. As he came inside the fence, he definitely heard someone say in a gasping voice, "Th...th...this is awful. Is anyone here? Anybody?"

The voice belonged to the elderly gardener Gonsuke.

When Kuroki pushed the back gate open, jumped to the side, and rushed in, Gonsuke had fallen back onto his butt on the ground and was mumbling like a goldfish tired of wheat bran. He could not find his voice and alternately thrust out the index fingers of both hands. He was pointing at the storehouse enclosed by an iron fence directly in front of him.

"Ah!"

Kuroki nearly fell on his backside, too. Above the vent of the storeroom, an eerie hole about two feet in diameter had been cut out and drew in the morning light.

Around that time, hearing the commotion many vassals of the clan came running.

"Thief! Thief!" they cried out but no villains were there to confuse.

Several of the main guards helped Kuroki. When they opened the large front door of the storehouse and entered to look around, there were no signs of three of the cedar chests, each filled with one thousand ryo, and stacked in a conical shape inside the storehouse.

You are probably familiar with one thousand ryo. A one-ryo koban gold coin of good quality at that time is just short of twenty yen in the gold market of today. If the economic situation or the current price is considered, it may be equivalent to more than one hundred yen. Therefore, one one-thousand-ryo chest would be worth ten thousand yen from the perspective of people today.

If one thousand koban coins weighing half an ounce each were placed in the chest, the equivalent weight would be thirty-two pounds. Then by adding the weight of the sturdy chest, the weight approached forty pounds. Fujioka Juro and Inuzuka Tomizo broke into the treasury of the Edo castle during the Ansei era (1854–1860) and carried off four one-thousand-ryo chests. Today, that story seems ridiculous. In that world, however, punishment for a theft of ten ryo was beheading. Therefore, this robbery was the biggest one since the rise of the Tokugawa shogunate.

The lower walls of oak and chestnut in Kuroki's storehouse were papered with sea cucumbers painted on top. The storehouse used as a treasury was broken into, and three chests were stolen. Obviously, these thieves were not ordinary. Seeing this, the money-grubbing Kuroki said, "Oh! This is terrible!" and fainted.

4

THE CHANGE Heiji DID NOT expect was theft and was with Garappachi at the time. During morning that day, he heard about the incident.

"I told you to keep watch there," said Heiji.

"The captain saw it all, and I'm very ashamed. Because Kuroki's fainting caused havoc, probably, the mansion was boiling over inside. I stayed at the home of Ushiya Kihei, my sworn brother in Sugamo. When I heard about the incident, I thought it would be a good idea to have an investigation. Because a poorly done job can't be reversed, I hurried back to tell you, Captain."

"It wouldn't be right to say you did good work. Your value to me is you're savvy where I'm inept."

"If you're gonna make fun of me after my hard work, it's hopeless."

"Don't get mad, Hachi. Well, are you coming?"

They got into two palanquins on the frosty streets of Edo and dashed to Sugamo.

Upon their arrival at Kuroki's estate, the detective Zenigata Heiji, who had a well-known face and name and had rushed there from Kanda, was given a warm reception by the vassals of the clan.

"The master?" asked Heiji wondering why he did not see the master Magoemon amid this commotion.

Someone said, "He's overwhelmed and is resting inside. He said to thank the captain for coming."

"Really?"

Heiji did not pursue meeting him.

His guide was the head clerk Tosaburo, a very wealthy manager. He was a young man of thirty who looked dignified and embodied the manager of a samurai family.

Heiji was shown around by Tosaburo. He meticulously investigated, regardless of difficulty, inside and outside the mansion, around the imposing earthen wall donated especially for the Jizo with human skin, the treasury inside the wall, the state of the cut-out hole, and the state of the storehouse entrance of the hallway leading from the bedroom of the master Magoemon.

"Who has a key to this storehouse?"

"It never leaves Master Magoemon's side."

"So the thief stole the key, opened the front door, and went in."

"That can't be so."

A cynical smile rose on Tosaburo's face. He probably thought it was too reckless for the thief to steal the key and go to the trouble of cutting through the tiled wall of the warehouse.

Heiji said, "Anyway, please summon everyone living in this residence to the garden. I'd like to question each one and look them in the face."

"..."

A smile rose again on Tosaburo's face and he withdrew without a word. At last, all the people living in the main building were side by side in the garden.

First, Kuroki Magoemon, who had been lying down until now, was a robust middle-aged man around fifty years old with graying sidelocks and a dazzling shaven part of his head. His avarice and energy were unrivaled. When he greeted Heiji again, his defeated spirit returned with the three-thousand-ryo blow, but somehow maintained the arrogance of a rich man.

Next, his mistress Sen was a pretty, twenty-five- or -six-year-old woman approaching middle age with a deliberate, sober character. However, she was an elegant woman with no suggestion of her past self. This was disturbing. And she wore no hint of morning make-up.

Shotaro, his first-born son and only child, was older than his mistress Sen. He sold herbal medicine in his store in Nihonbashi. He lived with his wife and many children at the store and rarely came to Sugamo, and still had not appeared.

Beginning with the head clerk Tosaburo, there were just fifteen or sixteen employees of both men and women. Each one seemed filled with greed, but not one seemed able to open a hole in the storehouse and steal three one-thousand-ryo chests.

"Is this everyone?"

"Yes," Tosaburo answered Heiji.

"Ume's not here," said the apparently wise Gonsuke.

"What! Ume, where is she?"

Heiji caught those words. He saw and understood Tosaburo's eye signal to not speak out of turn.

"It's nothing. Because she sleeps on the side of the storehouse, she's viewed a bit harshly because her voice cracked when she claimed she knew nothing. She's a stubborn girl and doesn't talk easily, but as a precaution, I'll bring her here," said Tosaburo clumsily hiding his embarrassment as he walked toward the storehouse.

From behind, Heiji said, "No, I'll go with you."

5

"OH! WHAT IS THIS?" ASKED a surprised Heiji. A fifteen- or sixteen-year-old girl was gagged and both arms were tied. She was suspended from a ceiling beam of a closet filled with garbage on the side of the storehouse.

Heiji should have seen this area but did not notice it until he saw the dimly lit ceiling beam.

When he lowered her, a dirty breeze descended with her. Mysteriously, her beauty radiated through the dust and dirt coating her.

"What is this about?" asked Heiji.

"It's nothing. She's always been a little light-fingered and is hard to manage in the house. Because she sleeps in this storehouse, she must know a thief entered last night. Some say this girl probably guided him in and enticed him. The master ordered that she be tied up for the time being and thoroughly investigated," said Tosaburo almost babbling.

"Is she the thief?"

"Yes, it looks that way."

When Heiji untied the girl and took her outside, Gonsuke, who tagged along, shouted with no compunction, "Captain, she's not the thief. That's what you said. Ume is the master's niece. Her older brother is wild and is missing. Sadly, Ume is treated more harshly than a servant. This story is about punishment."

"Quiet Gonsuke. This is none of your business," said Tosaburo.

"So you say, Mr. Head Clerk."

Nevertheless, Gonsuke felt a strong satisfaction and a slight smirk remained when he left to return to the garden. Heiji saved the girl and left with her.

She said, "Hey, Mr. Head Clerk, like the gardener said, I don't know anything."

"So you say."

"When you saw me, was my face the least bit malicious?" she asked.

"Does Captain Zenigata read faces, too?" asked Tosaburo.

Heiji was a little offended by the spiteful words.

Heiji asked, "I will ask you something seemingly irrelevant, but when you entered the storehouse this morning, you opened the door and entered with the master."

"What do you mean?" lashed out Tosaburo.

"Well, why is plaster stuck to your sidelocks?"

"What?!"

"Not just your sidelocks. Tosaburo-san, it's also stuck to your collar and obi. When I looked carefully, it was just a little, but dried plaster is dropping off. If you crawled through the hole in the storehouse, you would have brushed it off."

"Is plaster sticking to my body? Don't say such hateful things? If you have a truncheon and a policeman's rope, talk after you've searched a little more. If a hole were opened in the storehouse, wouldn't it be the head clerk's job to take a look?"

Tosaburo picked a fight. He seemed to hail from a samurai family and now worked here, and had the hallmarks of a man who was hard to deal with.

"I truly want to say I'm sorry, but Tosaburo-san, there's a tear in the side of your kimono from carrying a heavy object. Why is rust from metal there?"

"Huh!"

"From what you've heard, Master, do you have any objection to a search of the servants' rooms?"

Heiji had reached the garden and now ignored Tosaburo and turned his attention to Magoemon.

"If gold worth three-thousand ryo was taken out, you may search anywhere. Please search wherever you wish," said Magoemon.

"Hachi, please keep an eye on the head clerk. I will go inside and thoroughly search each room," said Heiji and stopped for a short time. Tosaburo's face was too placid and not the least bit disturbed by Heiji's words.

Heiji urged Magoemon to go inside while he assessed the situation in the area. For a short time, an air of tension and anxiety filled the garden, but Garappachi fully exercised his authority, and no one spoke.

Thirty minutes later, Heiji appeared on the veranda with an air of triumph and held a one-thousand-ryo chest at his side.

"Ah!" said Tosaburo who backed away.

Garappachi asked, "Are you gonna try to get away?"

Garappachi swiftly locked Tosaburo from behind. But one twist of his body sent Garappachi flying about six feet. Tosaburo, who was originally from a samurai family, had exhaustive knowledge of martial arts and the likes of Garappachi was no rival.

"Hachi, leave him to me. You can hold the woman."

When he pointed his chin toward the mistress Sen, Heiji's body flew through the air and a truncheon slammed into the shoulder of the fleeing Tosaburo.

6

"CAPTAIN, WHAT WAS THE REASON for that? Please draw me a picture like you always do. I'm completely in the dark," said Garappachi butting in as Heiji kept walking.

In the early afternoon of that day, Tosaburo and Sen were handed over to a disciple who ran up from behind, and the two leisurely left Sugamo.

"It's nothing. That head clerk Tosaburo conspired with the mistress Sen to open the vent in the storehouse. They schemed so it would look like a thief entered from the outside, but I noticed the niece Ume was treated cruelly and made to stay in the storehouse. They tried to hide this by hanging her from the ceiling beam and pretending not to know. It was useless work."

"Where did you find the one-thousand-ryo chest?"

"When I said I would search Tosaburo's room, he seemed calm. I thought that was strange and searched Sen's room because she signaled Tosaburo with her eyes. One chest was inside her wardrobe."

"Oh, so that's it. But what happened to the other two, since three chests were stolen?"

"They took them somewhere. Tosaburo hid each one."

"But Captain, it's not easy to hide three heavy chests in a very short time."

"You say curious things. Wait a minute. This may be my error," said Heiji and stood in the middle of the road lost in thought.

"Captain, people are staring and laughing. Let's go home."

"Wait, wait. My thinking may have been too shallow. Perhaps, the Jizo with human skin that caused an uproar a month before this major incident played some role."

"I don't know, Captain, but people will think you're crazy by standing in the road and looking lost."

"Garappachi, I'm going to start all over. Let's go."

"Okay."

"Tosaburo and Sen are small fry. Behind them is someone formidable," said Heiji as he left to return to Sugamo without delay.

They arrived at Kuroki's mansion around two in the afternoon. Ignoring the looks of surprise, Heiji searched one more time. He painstakingly searched inside and outside the estate, paying particular attention to the area near the Jizo with human skin. Around twilight, he had a revelation and turned to Garappachi in the middle of a yawn.

"Hachi, I got it."

"Really, you know where those other two chests are?"

"No, I didn't realize it until now, but I made a serious mistake."

"What?"

"For future reference, look at that pole. I was distracted by the stone Jizo-sama and didn't notice the pole.

Heiji came carrying a sturdy pole about eighteen feet long used to dry grain from the field outside the wall.

"The two one-thousand-ryo chests were tied to one end of this pole; the other end hung over to the other side of the wall. When I went around to the other side and pulled the rope attached to the front of the pole from the outside, I raised Jizo-sama. Because the stone Jizo-sama is rather heavy, the logic probably was to use the pole to draw each one-thousand-ryo chest closer and take it over the wall."

"So you figured that out."

"I climbed on the wall over there, passed the chest up here, and without making much noise, I smoothly slid the two chests down into the field."

"Of course."

"The heavy object was placed where the footprints of the pilgrims crossed in the field. There are probably square impressions and marks left by the rope."

"Oh."

"Parts of the top of the earthen wall crumbled a little."

"That's where the thieves entered from the outside."

"Yes."

"Were they Tosaburo and Sen?"

"That is where I'm totally puzzled. After the thieves stole and fled with the two chests, they later rendezvoused with Tosaburo and Sen at some convenient time. When seen under the moonlight, a hole was opened in the storehouse. Inside, the one-thousand-ryo chests were stacked in a conical shape. They blamed the crime on a thief, and took one chest, this kind of favorable circumstance is rare. As I said, Tosaburo is from a samurai family and had the courage for that kind of work."

"You saw that, Captain."

"If I hadn't thought of that, nothing would add up. Tosaburo and Sen were given the thief's surplus. Each one was prepared and rushed out of here."

"So who was the thief who came in from outside and stole two thousand ryo?"

"Wait, Hachi, you'll understand later."

Heiji raised his head and directed his gaze to the row of modest houses along the way to Sugamo.

7

"Is there a public bathhouse near here?"

"There is. At the corner where the road cuts through the middle of the field and opens into a wide road is the village bathhouse."

"Shall we go together?"

"Okay."

An odd tension ran down Garappachi's back muscles.

"Hello," said Heiji as he briskly stepped through the back door of the bathhouse. The light grew dim and the fire for the kettle faintly shone on the tall-paneled shoji screen.

"Who is it?" called a daring voice from inside.

"Is the attendant here?"

When the voice asked, "What's your business?" Heiji signaled Garappachi with his eyes and pulled open the shoji screen.

"You're under arrest!" he shouted and hurtled in.

"Huh, what is this?"

The bathhouse attendant tried to throw a bucket of boiling water for adjusting the bath temperature at Heiji. He dodged, raised his right hand, and struck the attendant's fist with a brass coin resembling a meteor.

"Yeow!" he said as the bucket dropped down, Heiji stepped in and quickly and forcibly tied up the attendant.

This happened so quickly the guests out front suspected nothing.

"You're not going to put up a fuss, are you?"

The proprietor heard the noise from inside and appeared, but was laid flat by a truncheon.

Heiji said, "Oh, I'm sorry, but I must borrow this man. For a short time, you will take over the clerk's job. Please don't alert anyone about this incident. All right?"

"Yes. Yes."

"Over there is a guest waiting to have his back sponged. All right?"

"Yes."

When the proprietor, who looked about to cry, shed his kimono, he used his experience learned long ago to become the bathhouse attendant and went out to the shop.

"Dammit! Talk! Tell me everything."

"I'm sorry, Captain. I wasn't being malicious. I owed a favor to someone from long ago."

The attendant started talking when threatened once with an expression lacking in ferocity. It was reasonable for Heiji to know from the pit of his stomach that the attendant wasn't a villain.

"Where is the person who asked for this favor?"

"I can't say even when only my cremated bones remain."

"All right. That's a good attitude. People have to be like that."

"Yes."

The attendant couldn't tell whether this was praise or blame.

"But that person you owe is probably far away."

"Oh?"

"Only you remain; they probably fled. Because they're carrying two thousand ryo, being tailed by you would have been a problem."

"That's…that's crazy. He's not that heartless. He still has business on that estate."

"Really? What?"

"What? He has other business there. What did he say?"

The attendant snapped his mouth shut, realizing he said a little too much.

8

AFTER MIDNIGHT THAT NIGHT, like floating up from inside the residence, someone clambered up the grim earthen wall right above the Jizo with human skin. Then another climbed up.

The first climber was an adult who was followed by a smaller figure, perhaps, a woman or a child.

The two caught their breath on the wall for a few moments. Finally, the first person, the larger climber, tied a rope to the waist of the smaller one, who crossed over the top of the wall and was slowly lowered down.

This was unexpectedly difficult work, but somehow it all ended safely. Next, the bigger person gently jumped down like a kitten from the wall, which was probably nine feet high.

Holding hands, the two walked straight down the field road and came out on the main road.

"Halt!"

Naturally, their path was blocked by Zenigata Heiji.

"…"

The two said nothing but had to be stopped from flying apart and taking big detours around him to the right and to the left. Heiji tried to chase down the smaller one but violently grappled with the shadow of the larger one.

"Don't resist!"

"Ah!"

Heiji adeptly handled the desperate fighter. When he pinned down the man, he signaled and Garappachi came flying in holding aloft a government-issued lantern.

"You got 'im Captain."

"Garappachi, perfect timing. Give me some light."

"There's another one here."

"That child got away."

When illuminated by the lantern held out by Garappachi, pinned under Heiji's knees was a dashing young man with a hand towel wrapped around his head and wearing a kimono with tiny indigo specks. When the towel was nearly ripped off, he saw a nice-looking but almost grim-looking man with a high nose, large eyes, and swarthy complexion.

"Oh, aren't you Goi Hide?"

"Ah, Captain Zenigata, I am ashamed."

"What is going on?"

Heiji lifted his villain to his feet and brushed the dirt off his body. Goisagi Hidekichi was a yakuza and a professional gambler with a criminal record, but he wasn't considered the type to commit serious crimes.

"I thought you only gambled, but in no time, you're mixed up in breaking into and robbing a storehouse."

"Captain, I understand why you see it that way, but I have a reason."

"Tell me."

Before they knew it, the four entered the thicket and were surrounded by red lanterns on the withered grass.

"The man captured by Captain Zenigata is very happy. What am I hiding? I am Hidekichi, the nephew of Kuroki."

"What? I heard you were a child of people with status, but I didn't know you were the nephew of the wealthy Kuroki. What is going on?"

Heiji's curiosity was burning.

Goisagi Hide's story was mundane but novel. When his father died, Hidekichi had too much fun, joined the yakuza, and cut ties with his family. His mother and his sister Ume were fairly well off and taken in by Kuroki Magoemon, his uncle. However, after his mother died, the despicable Magoemon embezzled her entire fortune of several thousand ryo she brought with her and cruelly sent away his younger sister Ume to starve.

Hidekichi negotiated many times for Magoemon to return the fortune and to take his sister back in, but Magoemon's excuse was his parents died without allowing the disinheritance and handed over nothing.

At that time, he heard his sister's life was precarious. Impatient, he got close to a long-time attendant working at the neighborhood bathhouse and wrote this absurd play. Last night, they broke into the storehouse and made off with two one-thousand-ryo chests. He did not know where his sister was and worried about her. And tonight, he entered to save her.

"That is my reason, Captain. My parent's money embezzled by my uncle Magoemon was not three or four thousand ryo, but a huge loss, probably twenty thousand ryo. I sent this money and my sister Ume to the home of a kind nursemaid, who lives in Meguro. I intended to humbly introduce myself. Captain, can you please overlook this?"

"…"

"The two thousand ryo does not belong to my uncle. I don't care one bit about funds for gambling. Captain, please look at my sister's predicament. Her circumstance is worse than that of a beggar child, but isn't she the niece of the wealthy Kuroki and is disgraced at fifteen in the bloom of her youth?"

Goisagi Hide's head hung down as he wiped away his tears. His sister Ume with a tearstained face was hunched over far from the light of the lanterns.

"Hide, I understand. If you take this chance to return to being an honest man, I will know nothing. The chests of gold may be boiling in a hot-water kettle, go quickly," said Heiji.

"You know that, too?"

"I understood almost everything."

"Thank you, Captain. I am indebted to you."

"No, never mind."

Heiji nudged Garappachi, who without looking back, set off for Edo.

"CAPTAIN, THERE'S ONE THING I don't get."

"What is it, Garappachi?"

"Why did you charge into the bathhouse and tie up the attendant?"

"As usual, you're easily tricked. Jizo-sama was warmed up every morning. If a bonfire wasn't started, wouldn't scalding with water be effective?

"Oh."

"When I sniffed that Jizo-sama, it gave off the scent of the bath in a public bathhouse."

"Ahah, but wasn't that a lot of trouble to go to?"

"Because there was no way to get closer to the earthen wall in the field, he thought the warm Jizo-sama would cause an uproar among the villagers giving him the chance to spy on this situation on the estate during the turmoil."

"Oh."

"Brass and worthless coins being transformed into silver nuggets was Hide's handiwork. He wanted to find out what was going on in that mansion," said Heiji and, without hesitation, looked back at Garappachi.

CHAPTER TEN

THE SEVEN BRIDES

1

"HEY, HACHI."

"What, Captain?"

"Lend me your ears."

"Heh, heh, heh. If these ears are good, you may use them as much as you wish."

"No need to put on airs. You don't actually give me your ears, it's a figure of speech. The truth is I'd like to borrow your legs."

Although declared to be a famous catcher of criminals, the detective Zenigata Heiji rarely tied one up. He left this up to his follower Garappachi now lounging under the sun.

The New Year's pine decorations had been taken down. The early afternoon was unusually warm and felt like the lingering drunkenness from spiced sake on the streets of Edo. After showing a middle-aged customer out, Heiji immediately went around to the veranda to wake Garappachi from his nap.

"Hey, where are we off to?"

"You probably overheard that conversation. That customer had a lot to say."

"Nope."

"You didn't hear?"

"I don't listen to other people's conversations. I'm not that low."

"I want to say that's admirable, but the truth is you were napping."

"Well, if the sun's rays are warm, and my chest is cool and stiff, all I can do is fall asleep."

"You're full of surprises. All right, I'll go over the details."

"You'll do that for me?"

"Be quiet and listen."

"Okay."

Heiji's attitude possessed an unusual seriousness. Surprisingly, the often-hopeless Garappachi kept his mouth shut and looked up at him.

"I just met with the proprietor of Yaotoku, a doll shop in Jukkendana. His only daughter Osen married the heir to a family in the same business, an establishment called Yaomine in Suehirocho. He asked to borrow my strength."

"She's a modern girl who married him even though he's a bad sort."

"No, it's not that. Please listen. Recently, brides have been disappearing one after another from Kanda to Nihonbashi."

"I've heard about that. The brides, who went missing on their wedding nights, should have been with their husbands from sunset. What if there's another man she exchanged vows with, and they decided to elope that night? At the last moment, the woman gained unexpected courage."

"According to Yaotoku's proprietor, three brides have disappeared."

"Oddly enough, that makes sense."

"You can't say something like that so easily. Hachi, the disappearance of three brides within two to four weeks is a little suspicious."

"Hearing you say that, I guess so."

"Because any family obsesses over a daughter finding a man and running away, they're concerned about respectability and don't want it to become public. The proprietor of Yaotoku is burdened by the fear his daughter will disappear, too."

"Of course."

"So my request to you is…"

"You probably want me to sniff out any bug stuck to that girl Osen."

"It's not a disagreeable task. The Yaotoku proprietor trusts his daughter. And for now, I trust him. You will discreetly enter the wedding procession and keep watch for the night."

"Of course. I have a nasty role."

"Why do you say that, Hachi?"

"Instead of using smarts and money, patience is important. I'll follow the bride on that day from the time the bride and groom drink sake in the *san-san-ku-do* ceremony until they exchange cups of wine before entering their wedding bed. This is gonna be hard."

"Don't expect too much."

"Anyway, Captain, I'm single."

"So you're saying you're dissatisfied about watching that place because you're single."

"Well, I guess it can't be helped."

As Garappachi complained, various scenarios turned over in his head about the adventure that night.

2

TODAY, A QUICK TRIP by automobile from Jukkendana in Nihonbashi to Suehirocho in Kanda takes around fifteen minutes. A wedding procession long ago would not have been so easy.

Five specially tailored palanquins from Kagosei in town carried the bride, the matchmaker couple, the bride's escort, and the important relatives. Following them and stretching across the street, people walked as they pleased and held lanterns emblazoned with the family crest. In these frightening times, the plan was for only the palanquins to fly by and the caterers to follow at their leisure. The five palanquins shouldered by young men selected for being swift runners stepped out to the streets of Edo on a frosty evening and ran to Nezuyayokocho from Myojinshita.

Suddenly, a pole came flying out of the darkness and landed between the legs of the lead palanquin bearer of the center palanquin carrying the bride.

"Ah! What the hell?" he said as the palanquin fell forward spectacularly, gained momentum, and dropped with a thud in the middle of the road.

"It came from over there," said the young rear palanquin bearer and took his staff and stood it at the front of the palanquin carrying the bride. His attacker ran out from the side to block him and thrust out to strike him in the chest.

In this skirmish in the twilight dusk, the villain had amazing dexterity, and the rear palanquin bearer automatically leaped up and landed on his backside. Meanwhile, without saying a word, second and third men seized the bride's palanquin and dragged it into a narrow side alley.

"Damn you stop!"

The front bearer finally stood up, but his leg was hit hard and he moved slowly. The other four palanquins in front and behind were set down. The eight youths asked, "What's going on?"

They brandished their staffs and fanned out in all directions in search of the bride's palanquin. Fortunately, the alley was a three-feet-wide bypass not easily passable by a palanquin. The bride's palanquin was slightly tipped over and blocked the entrance. The ten men had pluck and swinging ten staffs immediately began their chase.

Garappachi hired a town palanquin to follow right behind the bride's procession. He witnessed the commotion and jumped out almost overturning his palanquin.

"Did he finally come out? He won't escape."

This was business and he ran into the entrance of the first alley. The bride's palanquin instantly plugged the entrance, and the scoundrel could not be followed.

"Damn, this is in the way."

When they clambered over the palanquin and entered the dark alley, their way was blocked by a fearsome, solid wood door.

"I'll open it here."

He pushed and banged, but it did not budge.

First, the matchmaker couple and the escorts got out of the four palanquins over concern about the bride's safety.

"Osen-san, you were probably surprised," one said as they pushed up the straw curtain of the palanquin to look in, but the palanquin was empty.

"Oh no!"

The bride had been kidnapped.

3

SEEING THAT THEIR SCHEME enabled them to make their way close to Yaomine, target some gap in attention, and use the trick of using a byway to block its entrance with the palanquin, these scoundrels were not ordinary.

"Captain, I'm so sorry, I want to slice open my stomach."

To soothe Hachi who reported his humiliation, Heiji said, "No, in that situation, I may have failed if I had gone. Although I was in the middle of a job, it was my mistake to send you alone."

Without delay, he rushed from the byway of Nezumiya alley to Yaotoku in Jukkendana. He questioned each of the enraged people from Yaomine but did not find a single lead.

The rumor heard most often was "It took skill to throw a six-foot-long pole between the legs of the young man. This wasn't an ordinary thief or kidnapper."

Heiji left near daybreak without uncovering anything.

In those days, the gatekeepers for various daimyos and the guards at the approaches to castle gates, samurai attendants, and even low-status samurai used poles as a weapon. A trained man could throw a pole at the crotch of the palanquin bearer.

The bride, reputed to be a wise young woman, and the eldest son of Yaomine, her fiance, did not travel the path of romance. This was the gossip among the housewives.

She was the fourth stolen bride since the end of the year. The method differed each time. The perceptive Heiji was certain these crimes had been well planned.

Then during the morning three days later...

"Captain, have you heard?" Garappachi came shouting.

"What is it, Hachi? You're always making a racket."

"Ishihara's made a huge blunder."

"What?"

"Last night, while Captain Ishihara Risuke was keeping watch on the Yanagiwara riverbank, the fifth bride was kidnapped. She is the daughter of Mikuraya by the riverbank in Zaimoku. This looks pretty important."

"Hmm."

"It's fifty-fifty. Even Ishihara is made a fool. Hachigoro isn't the only one who fails. It's quite a spectacle."

"You idiot."

"Huh?"

"You say Ishihara failed and that becomes your excuse for failing?"

"Oh."

"I can't stand people with that attitude. You are you and Ishihara is Ishihara. I don't want a fool who cheers another man's failure around me."

"Oh."

"You're the sort who's too frank and doesn't have good results, but has the merit of not being the least bit malicious."

"Oh."

In a flash, Heiji's anger boiled over. In this situation, the shocked Garappachi remained silent for a time.

"Well, if you want to come, I don't want to see that wrong-headed fellow."

"Captain, thinking about what you said, I was wrong. Please forgive me."

"I can't."

"Don't say that Captain."

"If you want to apologize, it should be to Ishihara."

"..."

"If you're confused, I'll sweep your legs out from under you. If you take joy in Ishihara's great achievements, we'll meet again."

Did Garappachi look too surprised? He bowed two or three times, retreated like a frightened kitten, and hurried outside the lattice.

The usually mild-mannered Heiji probably had reasons for his anger. The kindhearted Garappachi lacked the courage to push back with a question and disappeared somewhere with a sadness he could not banish.

4

A SHORT TIME LATER the sixth bride was abducted. She was the daughter of a textile dyer in Shinkawayacho and married to the sake dealer Isenao in Kandanabecho. She was switched somehow on the way to Kandanabecho. When her bridal silk headdress was removed, the bride was another woman.

Her matchmaker never let go of the bride's hand until she entered the palanquin. She traveled to Isenao under the heavy guard of the tradesmen, who came and went at the time, by order of their boss. When the palanquin was lowered, in addition to the matchmaker, a large crowd formed, so there should have been no opportunity to make the switch during the journey.

What happened? On that night, by request from both families, Zenigata Heiji was sent out to watch the bride beginning in the evening. He never lost sight of her headdress, not for a moment.

The bride Tatsu could not have been switched while in the dye shop of the bride's family. But how was she switched? Even Heiji discovered nothing.

Instead of Tatsu, the woman made up to be the bride was Roku, a beggar who came out of nowhere two or three years ago and wandered Kanda. No matter what she was asked, she only rambled.

"Where did you come from and who brought you here? Will you tell me?"

"Can't say."

"If you don't tell me, I'll make you. You're hopelessly stupid."

Then more joined in to bully her.

"Even if you don't want to talk, can you at least tell us who told you that you'd become the bride of the young master Isenao?"

This situation was absurd.

She did not resemble the popular Tatsu and was older than thirty. Even without the bridal headdress, Roku would never be mistaken for Tatsu. Roku was a beggar, thin, and did not talk, but no one realized who she was until she was escorted to Isenao.

A more serious cause was the fear instilled by recent ominous rumors. People became nervous and may have been overtaken by unexpected psychological failures. Isenao was so upset he seethed and screamed at Heiji and, this time, lost respect for him.

Roku was arrested, bullied, and cajoled. When they tried blaming her nonstop the entire night, they only drew out, "A stranger came and said you're gonna marry the young master Isenao and dragged me to some strange house."

Roku's lack of brains only led to confusion the closer she was questioned. They didn't learn the identity of this stranger or the location of this strange house.

What was known was Roku's kimono with a family crest and obi sash had the identical color and pattern of the kimono worn by Tatsu. In fact, similar items prepared for Tatsu's marriage were among the items worn by the five kidnapped brides. If anyone had been paying the least bit of attention, someone would have noticed the difference.

"Captain Zenigata, as you see, it's over. It's no one's fault, but please search for the brides. If you look for the six brides together, no case takes precedence over this one. If there's the slightest chance..." Isenao choked on his words.

"I am ashamed. You are counting on me and I will search for them. I want to say in three days, but at best it will be in five days, in the middle of this month," said Heiji gently and determined in his heart to risk his life. With the feeling of being talked about behind his back, Heiji left. Neighbors, who heard the commotion, created a wall along the road. A haughty murmur moved through the darkness like a soft breeze.

5

"IS YOUR MOTHER HOME?"

"Oh, Captain," said Shizu and leaped up to greet Heiji. After becoming his fiancee, she stopped going out to the roadside teahouse in Ryogoku but went to the home of Sasano Shinsaburo, the police sergeant in Hatchobori. At most, she helped when they were shorthanded. Usually, she stayed at home to prepare for her wedding with her mother by spending many days holding a needle.

At that time, Shizu at eighteen years old was nine years younger than Heiji. She intended to finish the goblets for the wedding ceremony and pay respects to the matchmaker before the unlucky year arrived. Often out on official business, Heiji kept procrastinating.

When the always beautiful, intelligent, and kind Shizu looked at Heiji, she began to blush as she stood to welcome him.

"Oh, Captain, welcome."

In the next instant, her mother appeared.

Heiji said, "It has been a while. You look wonderful, but I'm not doing so well. However, I came today to ask for a little favor. This is perfect because I'd like Shizu to hear this, too."

"Well, being so busy is hard on you. So please tell us how we can be useful?"

"It's not so bad. The truth is it's not a nice story like helping an old person walk," said Heiji with difficulty and stroked his cheek.

"..."

Heiji said, "This would be reasonable coming from a matchmaker, but my feelings are inexcusable."

"..."

The mother and daughter looked at each other in silence. Heiji's true intention seemed to have consequences, but they did not understand him.

"I'll speak plainly, I have a reason for delaying marriage to Shizu. I think I want it to take place within this month. What do you think?"

"What?! This is not a case of the earlier, the better. Shizu and I thank you for wanting to do so, but we aren't too happy."

Shizu cast her eyes down, and her mother blushed a deep red and said, "And there are only three days left in this month. Captain, it will be impossible to prepare in time."

"Mother, I understand, but if we don't carry out a sham marriage ceremony within the next three days, I will no longer be able to face the world as a man."

"As a man, Captain?"

"You wouldn't understand if I told you, but as you know, brides have been stolen recently. The villains only targeted weddings throughout Kanda and several towns in Nihonbashi. Six brides were kidnapped in the evening. Were they spirited away or kidnapped? This is not a simple situation."

"That's true, Captain."

"Sasano-sama will also be very worried and may ask, 'What are you thinking, Heiji?' This is too vague and preposterous. The explanation of being spirited away is illogical to government authorities. As a man who carries a truncheon and a rope, I am sure this is the work of scoundrels."

"..."

"I'm aware that both Garappachi and Ishihara failed. It was a good idea for me to watch over Isenao's wedding, but I was outsmarted and had to admit defeat."

"…"

"I lack the spirit to go outside. I feel like the world is talking about me behind my back. Mother, I am asking this favor of you."

"…"

"My reason is frightening. This neighborhood has no weddings. While I'm delaying, my opponent has not given up. He may be gathering together the six brides to kill them. No, he wouldn't go that far. I wouldn't know what to do if they were carried off to a distant land. I need one more wedding to force my rival to make another move in order to obtain solid proof."

"…"

"My rival switched the bride right before my eyes. If I take a bride, there's not the slightest chance he'll watch in silence. It's distressing to think about the dangers to Shizu, but I should be able to uncover the villain's hideout for the first time with this kidnapped bride."

Heiji's earnest plea caused a cold sweat to break out on his forehead. Shizu's mother did not respond to his grave request. For a time, her neck with gray-flecked hair was buried in her collar as she thought. Whatever she was thinking lasted a long time.

"Captain, if it's that important to you, please use me."

She did not speak about the marriage, but Shizu looked up. Of course, her mother's feelings were harder to read than Heiji's

He asked, "Shizu, is there anything you wish to say?"

"No, my mother's concerns are absolutely right. I believe in your ability with all my heart. The time you raided the herbal medicine garden at the Takada Palace, the time I was suspended below the abandoned shack in Ochanomizu, didn't you miraculously save me, Captain? Tonight please use Mother and me, too."

Shizu placed a hand on her mother's knees and gently shook them to pester her a little like a spoiled child. Heiji was struck by the heroic spirit of this young woman and remained silent; he seemed to want to put his hands together and bow.

6

TWO DAYS LATER, HEIJI raised the goblets in the marriage ceremony to Shizu. The matchmaker was planning to marry a bride to the steward of Sasano Shinsaburo, the elderly Odajima Denzo, in the spring and was working hard at scattered preparations for their wedding. While the preparations were poor, they were complete.

Neither a palanquin nor a carriage could travel the two or three blocks from Shizu's home to Heiji's home. Strong regrets were not heard from Heiji and Shizu. It was still evening when in addition to old Odajima Denzo and his bride, a couple of Heiji's colleagues and followers formed a wide circle around the bride Shizu and escorted her to Heiji's home.

If Garappachi were present, Heiji thought he would probably be livening up the crowd in a wild voice. Loneliness blew like a cold wind into Heiji's heart. He anticipated the machinations of his unseen rival and burned with a fighting spirit.

Heiji intended his new wife to be kidnapped, and Shizu intended to be kidnapped from the heart of her wedding. The guests, who vaguely read the couple's feelings, found this wedding to be a true mystery.

Heiji's home was in an alley. Although he possessed wisdom and a chivalrous spirit, he had little money. Nevertheless, he scrupulously investigated the preparations for welcoming his bride, although borrowed, he managed in these hard times to gather a folding screen to set up, an ornamental Isle of Eternal Youth stand as decoration, and a hodgepodge of items like dining trays, silk-like seating cushions, and even braziers.

The party gathered in his row house where a ten-feet-wide room was used as the marriage hall. The back room served as the bride's preparation room. When the happy exchange of cups of sake by the bride and groom was over, the auspicious tune of *Takasago and Tofu* began.

Dressed in his kimono with his family crest, Heiji looked grand, but more than that, his bride looked exquisite. If the party adjourned in this state, everything would have been all right. Perhaps, the kidnapper of the six brides would not try to kidnap Zenigata Heiji's bride.

Finally, the bride entered the adjoining room. While feeling uncertain, Heiji changed out of his kimono. The cups made several rounds. The boisterous party forgot about the kidnapping and felt festive. After some time passed, no one saw Shizu.

"Excuse me," the hairdresser Tsuru peeked out from behind the folding screen to call to the old man Odajima, "Where is the bride?"

"I haven't seen her for a while," he said.

"What?"

The rattled party leaped to their feet. In an instant, the drunks sobered up as if someone snatched away the cloth covering one's face while relaxing in the bath.

"She changed clothes and went to the toilet. I haven't seen her since."

The master hairdresser Tsuru had a strawberry birthmark from her forehead to her right eye and was well known in the neighborhood. Her homely face distorted with worry.

"They've done it."

The groom Heiji cast off his haori coat and charged out to the back garden in only his socks. Someone had opened or removed the wicket gate to the alley. Even with night eyes in dim light, he spied one dropped ornamental tortoise-shell hairpin.

7

HEIJI'S ACTIVITY RESEMBLED an outbreak of fire. He bet everything to save the six brides. If more failures piled up, even if he died, it would be inexcusable.

Shizu's mother managed to hide her grief for a short time with the support of Sasano Shinsaburo. When he thought about Shizu's pure, beautiful body thrown into the jaws of death for his sake, Heiji felt a shiver rise from the depths of his heart, like her entire fortune had been invested in a roll of the dice.

Heiji had never taken this lightly but now made another desperate start to begin investigating all businesses related to the marriage. He targeted every logical business beginning with the dry-goods shops Echigoya and Shirokiya. He had no idea how many weddings were held every day in Edo but only discovered that it was pointless to choose only dry-goods shops in Nihonbashi and Kanda to make inquiries.

Next, Heiji and his men went around to dried-bonito shops, haberdashers, cabinet shops, various secondhand shops, snack shops, sake dealers, and any shop in the business of marriage. However, nothing suspicious turned up. There was not one rumor of anyone going around asking about wedding dates.

Heiji was well aware that the plot for kidnapping seven brides had been meticulously planned over a long time. This was not a chance encounter or haphazard work.

As a precaution, he had given up on the beggar Roku but thought he should go and inspect the abandoned, half-built storage shed behind Myoujin Shrine, which was her lair. He found her cruelly hanged to death and her unsightly corpse laying on rags and waste straw.

"Dammit. Since she ended so miserably, I should have asked her a little more."

Only this time, Zenigata Heiji had no idea what to do.

Heiji sent his men to make inquiries at the pawnshops and the antique shops all over downtown, but by evening, not one person had taken in any bridal articles.

While they continued their futile efforts, the sole realization was Ishihara Risuke and Garappachi's quest was nearly identical to Heiji's.

8

HEIJI GAVE SHIZU CAREFUL instructions on various matters, but mysteriously, the kidnapped Shizu left no signals.

Shizu wrote several notes addressed to Heiji and stuck them in her collar or obi sash to push them into the gaps of a lattice or a storm shutter. However, she did not deliver even one to Heiji from wherever she was confined.

Not only that, Shizu should have hidden several small bamboo flutes in her obi sash and in her pockets. If she continuously played a flute, even if the sounds never reached the ears of Heiji's men, the neighbors would consider the event strange and would spread gossip beside the wells.

Day and night, Heiji wandered everywhere from Kanda to Nihonbashi. He was taken aback by tissue paper dropped onto the street, recoiled at the sound of a masseur's flute, and ran around like a crazy dog.

All his efforts were fruitless. Heiji could neither rest nor sleep and was tortured by the horrifying vision of the corpse of the beautiful Shizu joining those of the other six brides floating down the Ogawa River on this day.

He was pushed forward by the terrible regret gnawing at him. He dragged his weary legs from behind the temple and over Shohei-bashi Bridge to Yanagiwara. From behind him, a hand was gently placed on his slumping shoulder.

"Captain, you are worried."

Heiji turned and glimpsed the hairdresser Tsuru. A kindly smile appeared on her homely face to comfort him.

"Ah, Tsuru-san?"

Heiji stopped as if in a dream.

"Have you learned anything about Shizu-san's whereabouts?"

Strands of her hair were held in place by a hairpin. Her black silk obi sash tied her collared *kosode* robe and hung down behind her with a touch of playfulness.

"I'm stumped, Tsuru-san. Do you have any ideas?"

"Ha, ha, ha. It's troubling to hear Captain Zenigata talk like that, but this time it's truly wretched."

Pretending to listen to her kind but cynical words, Heiji escorted Tsuru home.

"Will you come in for a cup of tea?" she asked.

"Thank you. Would you let me rest here for a short time?"

Heiji thought she would refuse, but she slid open the fine lattice door to invite him in.

The interior looked like the home of a widow. The furniture was polished. From inside, a few of her hairdresser's assistants stared as young women do, like the sight of a male guest was a curiosity.

"The tea's a bit weak," she said.

Heiji drew the tea, took a sip, and then set it down on the fireside board beside the oblong brazier.

"Do the young women stay here at night, too?"

"No, when there's no work, they go home at dusk."

"One or two must live here."

"With my disposition, I could never look after other people's daughters. They all go home."

"You are alone at night, Tsuru-san."

"Yes."

"This is the perfect situation. From now on, I will visit often."

"Oh, you're joking. It's naughty to talk like that because I'm a lady."

"Be that as it may, why don't you drop the facade and confess?"

"What? What are you saying?"

Tsuru suddenly became stern.

"Will you bring out the seven brides?"

9

HEIJI'S HAND SHOT OUT to grab hold of Tsuru's left wrist.

"What are you doing? Stop it. If you're playing, this is inexcusable for a police officer," she said, but he yanked her arm and drew her closer. A deep red folded-paper crane was chiseled in her upper arm.

"Tancho Tsuru, you are under arrest!"

"What?"

Out of nowhere, a dagger flashed in Tsuru's hand and was rapidly pressed against Heiji's throat. He knocked the dagger from her hand to the floor below her knees.

"I found you suspicious almost from the start, but I could not rush in without proof. Although seven brides disappeared one after another, did you think I would not suspect the hairdressers?"

As Heiji spoke, he pulled out his rope and swiftly bound her hands and arms.

"What are you doing? I'm a woman's hairdresser and known throughout downtown. What proof do you, a man called Zenigata, have to arrest me?"

Her red birthmark licking the tatami burned like fire. The bitter eyes of the homely woman blazed like a venomous serpent.

"Silence! Look at that wall. Those marks like snake eyes are scratched here and there by fingernails. They are signals from Shizu and suggest the zenigata coin in my name. I'm certain Shizu made them. Now, tell me where the seven brides are hidden."

"I don't know. I don't know. If you're searching for her, out back is the Kanda River, so taking a look at the bottom of the water would be a good idea."

Tsuru spoke these malicious words barely containing her anger and looking up with hate at Heiji.

He said, "If you don't speak, the seven will not be saved. People will lose faith in me, but your body will be killed piece by piece. Well?"

Heiji's power was exhausted. When his hand wiped off the cold sweat pouring down, he picked up the dagger dropped from the woman's hand and pressed it against her neck.

"Ah, it's cold and feels quite nice. Please be quick. If you kill me, I will be satisfied. Now, I will tell you something that is true. For a long time, I've held a secret love for you."

She seemed to be telling the truth. A mysterious passion burst in the eyes of the wicked woman looking up at Heiji.

"What?! You're a stubborn woman. Tell me! Where are the seven brides?"

As he shivered, Heiji flipped the dagger around and knocked the woman in her forehead.

"This is no good. While you're talking, the plan of gathering together those seven women and sending them out of Edo is happening. I will probably be executed, but instead of putting my head on display, the seven brides beginning with Shizu will be sold at a bargain in Shimabara, or maybe, Nagasaki."

"What? Send them all out of Edo."

Heiji opened the sliding door covered in a patterned design to the adjoining room. During this commotion, the assistant hairdressers disappeared. When he reached the last screen door, he was looking down at the swirling black waters of the Kanda River. For the first time, the final gleam of light to solve the riddle of this case shined on Heiji's chest.

10

"CAPTAIN ISHIHARA, FOR THE REASONS you said, I am ashamed and should stay here for now," said a disheartened Garappachi and placed both hands on the ground in front of Risuke.

"..."

Risuke said nothing and folded his arms. Heiji's indifference was easy to understand, but Risuke, who had been hostile for a long time, kept his look of satisfaction before Garappachi and fought against admitting defeat even a little.

"Anyhow, if I apologize, Captain Ishihara doesn't listen to me like Captain Zenigata. If you can, please step in and help me. To get me away from you, please hang me by my neck until I'm dead."

Seeing the seriousness of Garappachi's tone couched in his buffoonery, Risuke was tickled.

"Mmm, that's no good, what should we do? It would be best for you to stay here for a while."

"Thank you so much, Captain."

As they talked, two of Risuke's men approached.

"Captain, we've heard a strange rumor."

"What?"

"A scarlet silk crepe sleeve was snagged by a water guard at Ryogoku."

"What?"

"Not only that, over the past few days, strange objects like a yellow waistband and a waist cord of white-dappled deerskin floated to Hyappongui and Eitai."

"This is encouraging news. We must investigate. Hachi!"

Risuke stood up.

"We're all going."

"Beginning with Shizu-san, the seven brides are definitely crammed into a small house somewhere along the river."

Soon Risuke and Garappachi were in a skiff being rowed by the other men and looking in all directions around the river.

The day was over. At precisely this time, the *Tsukuba Oroshi* north winds swept across the gray waters.

Zenigata Heiji was rowing another skiff and searching the river. He ignored the homes from the banks from Hamacho to Komagata and only scrutinized the boats floating on the river.

The only way for the seven beautiful women to be gathered together and taken away unseen was by boat.

Upstream of the bridge, a houseboat rarely seen at that time was moored. Heiji looked again and again from a distance and was certain.

The houseboat he was watching raised its anchor and steadily left riding on the rising tide.

"Wait. Hold on. That boat is suspicious," called Heiji from the darkness and made the other skiff follow closely behind, and jumped from one boat to the other.

"What is this? Boats with men showed up," said the boatman as he lifted the pole and without warning started swinging. Heiji dodged the strikes.

When Heiji tried to reach into his pocket, the boatman's blow appeared to hit a vital point and easily bend him backwards into the water scale on the boat.

When he was about to jump in, a voice called out, "Who's making this racket?"

Three large, rough men flew out from the bowels of the boat. One man was a samurai.

"You are all under arrest. Don't resist."

"What?!"

"You kidnapped the seven brides."

"What? That...You're dead."

The three men lined up the tips of their swords and surrounded Heiji from three sides. Heiji's weapon was one truncheon.

The man who jumped in first pulled out a short sword. When Heiji tossed the truncheon from his right to left hand, his right hand reached into his pocket to retrieve a brass coin.

"Eeyaah!"

The coin hit the left eye of the man directly in front of him forcing him to retreat.

But two opponents remained. And two or three more boatmen rushed in from the bow to help.

Heiji alternated between swinging his truncheon and hurling coins. He was slightly off because his samurai rivals were unexpectedly expert and gradually put pressure on him.

As Risuke and Garappachi rowed their skiff from upstream to downstream, they spotted the danger encircling Heiji.

"Over there!"

They hit the bow of the houseboat.

Risuke shouted, "Zenigata, are you okay? It's Risuke!"

Garappachi shouted, "Captain, I'm here, too!"

"You're all under arrest!" shouted Risuke's men.

The fray continued for a while. Heiji and Risuke used the advanced arrest tactics employed when outnumbered. Not making any mistakes, the gang of five was soon bound hand and foot.

When they opened the divider and entered the hull of the boat, seven trembling brides were tied up in a clump looking like a crushed bouquet.

"Oh, Captain."

Among them was the most beautiful and sensible Shizu. When she saw Heiji, she jumped up as if awakened from a nightmare and ran to him.

THE HAIRDRESSER TSURU, the kidnapper of the seven brides, was the famous woman thief called Tancho Tsuru. The red birthmark from her forehead to her eyes was drawn with paint to help disguise her identity.

However, without the birthmark, she was a homely woman, older than thirty, and no man would glance at her. Originally, no one came with a marriage proposal. Her desperation and curses accumulated. She resolved to randomly kidnap the most beautiful brides in the world from their marriage ceremonies and make them plunge to the depth of misery from the peak of bliss.

Tsuru was aided by her accomplices and henchmen. They were arrested by Zenigata Heiji at the best time to transport the seven women at the height of their beauty to Shimabara or Nagasaki by boat and sell them. Of course, the scarlet silk crepe sleeve and the yellow waistband that floated to Ogawa was the clever work of Shizu.

Heiji took Garappachi to task with Risuke present. Needless to say, his real intention was to reconcile with his superior Risuke. This time, Risuke admitted to being defeated by Heiji and did not harbor a grudge.

CREDITS

Cover Images:
1. Famous Scenes of Edo - Scene of Saruwaka-cho (名所江戸百景　猿わか町よるの景), Hiroshige. Retrieved from the National Diet Library Digital Collections [http://dl.ndl.go.jp/info:ndljp/pid/1303296] (March 22, 2018).
2. Ming coin photo By No machine-readable author provided. Galopin~commonswiki assumed (based on copyright claims). - No machine-readable source provided. Own work assumed (based on copyright claims)., CC 表示-継承 3.0, https://commons.wikimedia.org/w/index.php?curid=780119
3. Famous Scenes of Edo - Scene of Okawabata, Ryogoku (両国橋大川ばた), Hiroshige. Retrieved from the National Diet Library Digital Collections [http://dl.ndl.go.jp/info:ndljp/pid/1303243] (May 5, 2018).

Coin Graphic:
svg By Mukai (Mukai's file) [GFDL (http://www.gnu.org/copyleft/fdl.html) or CC BY-SA 3.0 (http://creativecommons.org/licenses/by-sa/3.0)], via Wikimedia Commons

Japanese Text:
Nomura, Kodo. *Oru Yomimono* (オール讀物), Bungei Shunjusha, April 1931 to January 1932. Retrieved from Aozora Bunko (January 1, 2014).
Chapter 1 [https://www.aozora.gr.jp/cards/001670/card56372.html], April 1931.
Chapter 2 [https://www.aozora.gr.jp/cards/001670/card56278.html], May 1931.
Chapter 3 [https://www.aozora.gr.jp/cards/001670/card56314.html], June 1931.
Chapter 4 [https://www.aozora.gr.jp/cards/001670/card57231.html], July 1931.
Chapter 5 [https://www.aozora.gr.jp/cards/001670/card56220.html], August 1931.
Chapter 6 [https://www.aozora.gr.jp/cards/001670/card57233.html], September 1931.
Chapter 7 [https://www.aozora.gr.jp/cards/001670/card56383.html], October 1931.
Chapter 8 [https://www.aozora.gr.jp/cards/001670/card56347.html], November 1931.

Chapter 9 [https://www.aozora.gr.jp/cards/001670/card56318.html], December 1931.
Chapter 10 [https://www.aozora.gr.jp/cards/001670/card57216.html], January 1932.

ABOUT THE AUTHOR

KODO NOMURA (born Nomura Osakazu, October 15, 1882-April 14, 1963) was a Japanese novelist, composer, and music critic (Nomura Araebisu). He is best known as the author of *Zenigata Heiji Torimono-Hikae* (銭形平次捕物控) — the first story was published in 1931, and 383 stories were written over twenty-six years. He was born the second son to a farming family in Hikobe-mura (now Shiwa-cho), Shiwa-gun, Iwate Prefecture.

In high school, he introduced a younger student and future poet Ishikawa Takuboku to haiku and tanka. In 1907, he entered the Faculty of Law of the University of Tokyo, but withdrew for lack of funds and joined the political department of the *Hochisha* newspaper. He adopted the name Kodo when he published a serial column on personalities called *Jinruikan*. He also used the pen name Araebisu when he wrote as a record critic.

In 1949, he formed and was the first president of the Torimono Sakka Club. To contribute to education in his hometown, in 1956, he established the Kodo Library (now the Shiwa Town Library) in Hikobe, Shiwa-cho and donated his works to the library. As a record collector for over forty years, he amassed thirteen thousand records and donated ten thousand to the city of Tokyo in 1956. He died of pneumonia at his home in Kamitakaido, Suginami-ku, Tokyo.

From the Japanese Wikipedia page for Nomura Kodo (野村胡堂). (Retrieved April 27, 2018)

www.jpopbooks.com

82951215R00093

Made in the USA
Middletown, DE
08 August 2018